7

DANGEROUS
JOURNEY

The
DANGEROUS
JOURNEY

*The true and chilling crime of
attempted murder in 1840s England*

Frederick J Hillberg

BROWN
DOG
BOOKS

Published under licence by Brown Dog Books and
The Self-Publishing Partnership Ltd, 10b Greenway Farm, Bath Rd,
Wick, nr. Bath BS30 5RL, UK

www.selfpublishingpartnership.co.uk

ISBN paperback: 978–1–83952–820–0
ISBN e-book: 978–1–83952–822–4

Cover design by Kevin Rylands
Internal design by Mac Style

Printed and bound in the UK

This book is printed on FSC® certified paper

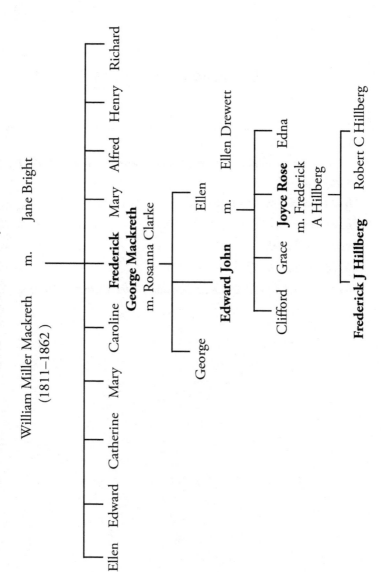

The Miller Mackreth Family Tree

William Miller Mackreth (1811–1862) m. Jane Bright

Ellen — Edward — Catherine — Mary — Caroline — **Frederick** Mary — Alfred — Henry — Richard

George Mackreth m. Rosanna Clarke

George — **Edward John** — Ellen m. Ellen Drewett

Clifford — Grace — **Joyce Rose** — Edna
m. Frederick A Hillberg

Frederick J Hillberg — Robert C Hillberg

Acknowledgements

I would like to thank Richard Tisdal, Author and Broadcaster for his inspiration
My Brother Robert for his research
The Hillberg Family
The Bright Family
The Mackreth Family
And my friend Jane Shergold at Carraway who made this happen.

Part One

Part One

Chapter 1

In the August of 1840, a young man in his thirtieth year, is about to embark on a business trip from Bristol to the Midlands. It is a journey he has made many times, but this time it would prove to be extraordinary and would alter his life forever.

At about five feet 11 inches, medium build, with black wavy hair and blue eyes, Mr William Miller Mackreth was an accountant at a Bristol lead shot[1] manufacturer who had just become engaged to a fair-haired young lady named Jane Bright, the daughter of a prominent Bristol family. Before they met, William had focused his attentions solely on his career and investments, but this changed when the couple had fallen in love at first sight and soon after received their families' blessings. Both smitten with each other, the two sweethearts simply could not wait to be married. William was sad to leave but was comforted by the fact that he would be back home in Clifton within a few days.

William waited with several other passengers on Small Street for the arrival of the Mail coach. He checked the Bristol Time[2] with his silver fob watch as he heard the bellow of the post horn and a clatter of wheels on the cobbles. His travelling companion was a jovial

---

1. Lead shot was manufactured for rifles and pistols. The production of perfectly round shot was invented in Bristol and involved dropping lead from a great height, known as a shot tower, through a shiv into cold water and the shot was formed.

2. The clock over the old Corn Exchange in Bristol has two minute hands. The red minute hand shows Greenwich Mean Time and the black minute hand shows Bristol time which was historically (before the advent of the railways) 10 minutes later than London to reflect the solar time difference. Greenwich Mean Time (GMT) did not become Britain's standard time until 1880.

ironmonger named Mr Gunning, and the two spent a pleasant time chatting about their respective trades. Both gentlemen were bound for Ludlow in Shropshire, an important fair for buying supplies and raw materials.

Ten hours later, after various stops, William arrived at a coaching inn in Birmingham, where he had booked a room for the night before continuing his onward journey to Shrewsbury, and then on to Ludlow the following day.

That evening, William and Mr Gunning spent several hours together in the Commercial Room, exchanging life's experiences over glasses of porter. Mr Gunning told William some risqué tales of his experiences with chambermaids during his extensive travels, despite being a happily married man with four children. William was no prude and enjoyed the stories, but he only had eyes for Jane. While Mr Gunning regaled his stories, William fondly recalled the gentle kiss he had stolen the previous night when her father was looking the other way. Mr Gunning was staying at another hostelry that evening, but they both agreed to look out for each other in the future.

The next day, William departed from Birmingham in the Red Rover Coach bound for Ludlow via Shrewsbury, unaware that a coincidentally named Mr Ludlow, a wealthy butcher and cattle dealer, would also be making the same journey. Mr Ludlow was known to carry a large amount of gold coin on him to make his purchases, and there was someone else extremely interested in Mr Ludlow's journey and who had every intention of relieving the gentleman of his gold by any means necessary.

The interested person was a young man of very slight build, about five feet eight inches tall, with deep brown eyes that held your attention like a snake. He was well dressed and polite, introducing himself as a Mr Josiah Mister from Birmingham, who was visiting a distant cousin. It was the first thing that had come into Mister's head as he had never been to Shrewsbury before and had not expected to be asked the question of his business. The complaint on the ever-rising cost of travel and living arose in some conversations, and once or twice the disastrous Afghan War came up, but no one wanted to dwell on British Army defeats. This was Great Britain and the Empire, after all. The subject of families was also discussed, and it all helped to pass the time on the journey to Shrewsbury.

After several hours of travelling by coach, they arrived at the Unicorn Inn in Shrewsbury, where Mr Ludlow was a well-known figure. Once booked into the Inn, Mister swiftly made a beeline to Mr Ludlow, introduced himself and asked him about his business and his purpose for visiting the fair

Shrewsbury was busier than usual because of the three-day fair that drew farmers and country folk from far and wide. The atmosphere in the town was lively, with friends and acquaintances meeting up to share gossip and business, get drunk, and meet women also looking for fun from their normal hum-drum lives. Many often returned home from the revelry with more than they bargained for.

After booking in for the night, Mister made a point of ingratiating himself with one of the older chambermaids at the inn called Polly. She was a well endowed woman who knew how to make ends meet. In addition to her meagre salary, she often provided companionship to the gentlemen who stayed at The Unicorn, visiting them late into the night. Even the landlord was not immune to her charms when his wife visited her mother on the other side of town. However, Mister stood out from the other guests as he was not interested in Polly's night-time services. He had no money but hoped to change his fortune very soon. Mister was after information, and Polly gave it to him without a second thought.

"Yes, I know Mr Ludlow. He's stayed here many times before. He is very generous," she said, remembering the occasional silver sixpence he had given her without asking for anything in return. "He normally stays in the same room, but this time he's sharing it with a friend who's come to meet him – a Mr Jobson."

Mister's plan to rob the wealthy Mr Ludlow was beginning to fall apart as he had assumed he would be sleeping alone. He needed to reconsider his next move. He decided to go down to the Commercial Room where most of the guests would typically go for a chat, a drink, to smoke, or play a game of cards. It was somewhere women travellers, who were far and few apart anyway, never ventured, as they were designated a separate parlour.

Upon entering, Mister immediately noticed his proposed victim, deep in convivial conversation with Mr Jobson. Mister ordered a tankard of porter and moved within earshot of the pair. What he heard lightened his depression, and he began to hatch a revised plan. Mr Ludlow was agreeing to meet Mr Jobson at his next port of call, the Ludlow Fair, which started in a couple of days.

Mister had arrived at the inn with no luggage of substance, making the landlady Mrs Goodwin suspicious. She was right. The next morning, he left the Unicorn Inn early before anyone was stirring, without paying his bill of £1 15s 10d and in haste left a few articles of clothing behind. His plan was to walk to Ludlow, living off his wits.

With not a penny to his name, he started the 27 mile journey to Ludlow. He hitched lifts, took shelter overnight in barns and hayricks, begged for food where he could and managed to arrive in Ludlow the day before the Fair.

It was about seven o'clock in the evening when Mister reached the outskirts of the town. In the summer evening light, he spotted two men fishing by the River Teme, farm workers by the way they were dressed in their smocks. They looked up as he approached, and although he was dressed as a young gentleman, his clothes looked a bit worn, yet they thought they might be able to get a copper or two from him.

"Evening sir," they said in unison.

"Good evening," he replied. "I was wondering if the Red Rover Coach from Birmingham was due?"

"Should be here before dark, I wouldn't wonder," said the short, fat, purple, florid-faced one, taking a swig from a large jug of cider before handing it to his friend.

"Thank you," said Mister and briskly walked away.

"Tight stuck-up bastard," said the fat one, loud enough for Mister to hear, but he took no notice, not having a farthing in his pocket anyway. Mister sat on a wall about a hundred yards from his destination, The Angel Coaching Inn[3] and sure enough, about an hour later, the Red Rover coach came rumbling up the cobbles with the post horn blaring.

---

3. The Angel Inn was situated at 8 Broad Street. The grade-II listed building dates from 1555 and is now used as a wine bar and restaurant. This major coaching inn was visited by Vice Admiral Lord Nelson.

Chapter 2

As soon as the stage passed Mister he sprinted after it, lagging just behind. As the passengers stepped out, Mister moved close to Mr Ludlow to give the appearance that they had travelled together.

The landlord of the Angel Inn heartily welcomed his old customer and assumed, as Mister had hoped, that he was a friend of Mr Ludlow. The landlord then escorted Mr Ludlow to his room that unfortunately he explained was not his usual room, due to the demand by visitors to the fair, but he assured him it was one of his best and up to the standards he would expect.

Meanwhile, Mister was shown to his room by a chambermaid called Nellie and immediately started trying his charm on the poor unsuspecting country girl, asking if she knew his travelling companion. Nellie replied that Mr Ludlow was a regular customer when the fairs were on and always stayed at The Angel in room number 17. He was a genuinely nice gentleman and always left a remuneration of at least a shilling, for which she was always grateful.

Mister had the information he wanted and cut the conversation short, going downstairs to the Commercial Room, where he was immediately recognised. "You are the young man from the Unicorn Inn at Shrewsbury," exclaimed Mr Ludlow. "Why not sit and join me for tea in another room?" Mister gladly accepted, as the tea and cake would be more than welcome as he had nothing pass his lips since a kindly farmer, who had caught him in his barn still asleep that morning, gave him some porter and bread and beef dripping for breakfast.

The evening wore on, and Mister gave little away, but Mr Ludlow did gather that he came from a middle-class Birmingham family. Mister did not let on that, in fact, he was the black sheep of the family and did not particularly care for work when he could make a living in other ways. Later, for supper, Mister dined on a farmer's ordinary[4] with wine, brandy, and cigars. Around half past ten, Mister excused himself and asked another one of the chambermaids to escort him to this room. Holding a candle, she guided him upstairs giving him another candle for his own use when reaching the door and wished him a good night.

Meanwhile, the young William Mackreth who had arrived at The Angel before Mr Ludlow, had since been visiting clients and making purchases on behalf of his company in Bristol, so he did not return to The Angel until 11 o'clock in the evening. When he arrived, the busy chambermaid called Nellie took his shoes to be cleaned by the boot boy and gave him a pair of slippers, then took him to his room up the same set of stairs to room number 17, the room that for many years had normally been reserved for Mr Ludlow. Due to the exceptionally busy time, the landlord, not wanting to lose business, had decided to give the room to William. Nellie had certainly noticed that this young man was a cut above the rest. He appeared well dressed, had a lovely smile, and was definitely handsome she thought. She felt herself blush like a schoolgirl and would certainly not say no should the opportunity arise and expect no reward in return. She would be disappointed however as William's heart belonged elsewhere.

William entered his room and locked the door behind him. Nellie turned around to leave and noticed that the door to number 20 was not closed tight and the light was showing. Thinking nothing more of it, Nellie returned to her own room, slightly downcast that her favours were not required. Nellie attracted plenty of attention

---

4. A hearty set meal of the day typically starting with soup, followed by a pie or savoury pudding, roast meat or poultry.

from the male visitors, some welcome and some unwelcome, but she dared not complain if she wanted to keep her job. Even the landlord took advantage when the missus was not about.

The room was shrouded in darkness and William struggled to light a candle. He cursed himself for not taking an extra light from the chambermaid. Despite his exhaustion, he needed to make a few notes in his portable writing desk, which also had a secret compartment to keep his gold and silver coins for business transactions. After finishing his work, he changed into his night attire and climbed into bed, soon dreaming of his life back in Bristol and his forthcoming marriage to Jane.

Just a few hours later, William was suddenly awakened by a pressure under his chin and felt himself being violently pulled backward. He felt a strange sensation and instinctively put his hand to his face, only to find it disappeared into his mouth! He struggled with all his strength against the feeling of being gripped. His nightshirt was torn, and he managed to stand up. Although he could not see anything in the darkness, he felt a presence push past him. He stumbled towards the window, pulling at the curtains, and breaking a windowpane. He murmured a noise that sounded like "Fire! Murder!" even though his mouth and throat were fast filling up with blood.

The commotion began to alert the entire household as William stumbled towards the door, which was now unlocked. In that instant he was confused, as he distinctly remembered locking the room the night before, but the thought was soon displaced as he realised a liquid was pouring from his face. Hanging on to the banister for support, he managed to stagger down the stairs, getting weaker by the second.

Mr Cooke, the landlord, and the boot boy were the first to assist him. Everyone in the house was now awake and exiting their rooms to see what the noise was about. The group initially thought it was an attempted suicide, but William managed to gesture for paper and pen to write. They passed him a steel-nibbed pen and he started to scrawl: "Some villain has done it. Someone has tried to murder me!"

Chapter 3

The constables were called, and two renowned surgeons who were staying at the inn, a Mr Hedges, and a Mr Crawford, took charge and demanded that the room be cleared so they could administer their skills to William. The chambermaids brought hot water and linen, both visibly shaken by the events.

Mr Hedges skilfully stitched up William's face, which had been cut from ear to ear through the mouth, with a small part of his tongue now missing. There was also a puncture wound to his throat, which had just missed the windpipe and could have been fatal if it had penetrated another inch to the right. Dr Lloyd, the local physician, had also been called to the inn and his assistance was welcomed by his fellow medics.

"This gentleman has been very lucky," said Hedges.

"He will need a great deal of care if he is to survive. I have never seen anything like it in all my years as a physician," said Dr Lloyd. "And I hope never to again."

Mr Hedges would have looked after William for a few more days but had to continue his journey to Birmingham, so he was replaced by his colleague Mr Crawford.

There was a knock on the door. It was Mr Cooke, the landlord, followed by members of the local constabulary, who immediately started to examine the scene of the horrendous attack. Mr Hedges made it perfectly clear that, under no circumstances, was Mr Mackreth to be questioned. The poor man could not speak and was very weak from the loss of so much blood.

An officer was immediately dispatched to inform the local magistrates of the tragic events that would shake the whole town.

The leading Officer called Hammond noticed the broken window from which William had called for help. There were bloodstains on the curtains, the carpet, and the floorboards leading to the door. He noted that William was still wearing his torn nightshirt, which was naturally saturated with his own blood.

Officer Hammond felt a cold shudder go through his body. He had investigated many crimes in Ludlow, but nothing quite like this. The blood trail led down the stairs and walls, as he expected from the description of events already given to him by Mr Cooke. Returning to room 17, Officer Hammond noticed a number of spots of blood leading to the outside of room 20 down the corridor. A curious neighbour, a Mr Peach, had already followed the trail of blood and came to the same conclusion as the officer.

Officer Hammond returned to room 17 where Mr Hodges and Dr Lloyd were still attending to William, whose nightshirt had now been changed and most of the blood had been cleaned from his face and torso.

"What is your opinion of the weapon used, sirs?" asked Officer Hammond.

"A razor without a doubt," they both concurred. "The cut is too clean and fine for a knife."

"Do you have the razor, sirs?"

"No," said Mr Hodges. "I looked for one, expecting it to be on the floor, but Dr Lloyd found Mr Mackreth's unused razor in his washbasin drawer."

"Thank you, sirs," said Officer Hammond. "It's quite a mystery. I have some more questions for Mr Cooke, so please excuse me."

On leaving the room, Officer Hammond was apprehended by the inquisitive neighbour, Mr Peach, who lightly tugged on his coat sleeve and said, "Excuse me, officer."

"Yes, what can I do for you, sir?" replied Hammond, looking down from his six-foot height to a little rotund, rosy-cheeked face.

"My name is Harry Peach, and I live two doors away. When I heard all the noise and came to help, I noticed some blood leading from the gentlemen's room along the passageway, and I thought I should mention it."

"That's very observant of you." said Hammond in a slightly mocking voice, "and I will make a note of it you can be sure of that, and a Very Good Night to You, Mr Peach." hinting that he should now leave the inn.

A crestfallen Mr Peach made a swift exit wondering why he had not received more praise as a good citizen for his observations, but he would now go home and tell his wife and family about how useful his detective work had been to the constables. Over the next couple of months, he also benefited from many free tankards of porter while telling his tale in the local taverns. His yarn became more elaborate each time it was told.

Meanwhile, Mr Cooke was busy with the boot boy. His customers had been awake for a while, shouting for their cleaned boots and shoes.

"Mr Cooke," inquired Officer Hammond, "can you tell me the name of the patron in room number 20, please?"

"Certainly, sir," replied Mr Cooke. "He's a strange young man from Birmingham, but I cannot remember his name offhand. Come with me into the office, and I will check the register."

"Ah, there it is," said Mr Cooke, pointing to the lined book. "A Mr Josiah Mister from Birmingham. He is friendly with one of my regulars, who also comes from Birmingham, a Mr Ludlow, who deals in cattle buying at the fair."

"Who was the last person to see this fellow, Mister?" asked Officer Hammond.

"That would probably be Susan James," replied Mr Cooke. "She is one of my chambermaids, and she usually deals with that part of the landing. They share the duties between them in case there might be some benefits, if you know what I mean," he added, giving Hammond a knowing look. Officer Hammond knew only too well what he meant.

"Wait here; I will get her for you. She will probably be in the kitchen, helping with the breakfast," said Mr Cooke.

Susan, who was busy frying sausages, turned as Mr Cooke noisily came into the kitchen. "Officer Hammond wants to have a word with you but be quick about it. They will all be wanting their breakfasts," he said.

Susan ran out of the kitchen and almost bumped into the officer. "The guest staying in room 20. Did you see him up to his room last night?" asked Officer Hammond.

"Yes," replied Susan. "I took him up about half past ten and made sure he had all the amenities in his room, sir. He had about three inches of candle, a washbasin, a full jug of fresh water, a napkin, and a chamber pot. I then left the room and went downstairs for my supper."

"Thank you. That's all for now," said Hammond. Susan scurried back to the kitchen, hoping that the sausages had not been burnt.

"Can I be of any help to you, officer?" came a voice from behind.

Hammond spun around and saw a very distinguished gentleman. "Let me introduce myself. I am Mr Crawford of the medical profession. I am a guest of this inn and have just been in consultation with my colleagues attending to the unfortunate gentleman in room 17. It's quite a mystery, as the gentleman in question clearly did not inflict those wounds upon himself."

"I have noticed drops of blood leading to this room, and I am about to interview the occupant. Please join me," said Mr Crawford with authority.

Hammond knocked on the door of Room 20, but there was no reply. He tried the latch, which opened. There, under the bedclothes, lay a huddled figure.

Chapter 4

The figure stirred, and a gruff voice mumbled, "What do you want?"

"I would just like to ask you a few questions, sir. What time did you retire last night?" asked Hammond.

"At around half past ten. The chambermaid brought me to my room."

"Did you see anything unusual or out of the ordinary?"

"No, nothing," replied Mister as the bed sheets dropped from his person. Hammond and Mr Crawford noticed that he was clothed apart from his stockings and shoes. Hammond's sharp eyes also noticed a stain on the shoulder of Mister's shirt, which could be blood, and signs that an attempt had been made to remove other marks as well.

"I cannot find my stockings. That's why I am not fully dressed yet. I have been looking for them everywhere," exclaimed Mister.

"Excuse me one more time, sir," Hammond said and went to the landing to call for the two other officers who had accompanied him to investigate the case but had done nothing apart from becoming familiar with the housemaids hoping for some free food and payment for a few favours.

"I'm sure my Sergeant will soon arrive and expect some progress on what's been happening. The news of the horrific attack is now all over the town, and a crowd has begun to gather outside. You, Evans, go back downstairs and keep an eye on the crowd. You, Fenner, stay here. I will be back in a minute," Hammond said.

Hammond went back along the landing to room 17 and noticed that the door had not been forced, and they had not found a weapon. The doctor and surgeon were still attending to William. He then went back to room 20, where Mister was still sitting on the edge of the bed, looking quite relaxed and quite unperturbed by what was going on.

At the same time, Mr Crawford was scouring the room and his eagle eye noticed a stain on the curtain, which he was sure was blood. The window looked out onto the bakery yard next door.

"Officer Hammond, would you mind having a look at this?" Crawford asked.

Hammond had a look and was immediately of the same opinion that it was blood. There was also a dark reddish-brown mark on the window latch. "I will get the yard that belongs to a Mr Whatmore searched immediately. Fenner, you stay here, and see no one leaves or enters without my permission or the Sergeant when he arrives. I have some more questions to ask downstairs," Hammond said.

Hammond went looking for Edward Cooke, the landlord, who he soon found in the kitchen pressing himself against Susan James. She blushed and brushed down her skirts. Cooke looked unflustered and continued swigging his porter.

"How can I help you, Officer?" Cooke asked.

"I would like to speak to the person who took Mr Mackreth to his room when he retired yesterday evening, if that's possible," Hammond said.

"That would be our Nellie Winters. She's cleaning up the Commercial Room. That's her part of the landing. Susan, fetch Nellie, and be quick about it," Cooke said.

Susan hurried into the Commercial Room, "Aay Nellie, that copper wants to have a word with you now."

"Bother," said Nellie. "I wonder what he wants."

They hurried to the kitchen, where Officer Hammond was making small talk with Cooke. "Miss Winters, I believe you took the gentleman Mr Mackreth to his room last night. Did you notice anything unusual?"

"Not really," Nellie hesitated. "But come to think of it, I did see a light coming from number 20, which I did think odd as it meant the door was not properly closed."

"Thank you, Nellie. That is all. But if you think of anything else, please let me know," Hammond said, before she returned to her chores.

Hammond examined the door to room 20 before entering. Hammond's senior, a Sergeant Otley finally made an appearance and asked what had been discovered. Hammond explained about the bloodstains found in the hallway leading to room 20, the bloodstains on the shirt, window curtains, and latch. He also mentioned that he had ordered a search of Mr Whatmore's yard, which was directly below the window.

"Well done. I think we have enough to take the young man into custody for further questioning," Sergeant Otley said.

Just then, Officer Fenner appeared at the door. "We found this in the yard directly in line with this bedroom window, sir."

It was a black-handled cut-throat razor, partially wiped but still wet with blood.

Chapter 5

With the weight of the evidence beginning to mount, Josiah Mister was later led away to the local lock-up to await the pleasure of the local magistrates and prosecutors.

Hammond stayed in the room and was joined by Mr Crawford. Hammond had noticed that Mister was unshaven. All the water had gone from his jug and there was nothing in the washbowl. They looked in the drawer under the washstand and found no sign of a razor but wrapped in a small piece of cloth was a small, white, crystallised piece of stone.

In the 1840s, everyone was familiar with this type of stone. It was alum and was commonly used to remove bloodstains.

They continued to search the room and found the chamber pot quite full to the brim and not of the colour one would expect. Without hesitation and much to Hammond's surprise, Mr Crawford stuck a finger into the pot and put it to his mouth. "Alum, without a doubt," he declared.

Meanwhile, William had been carefully moved into another bedroom with Mr Crawford's permission to allow number 17 to be thoroughly examined while attendants recommended by Dr Lloyd had been summoned to attend William night and day.

Letters needed to be sent to William's family as a matter of urgency. The address of William's employer Christopher George, Harding and Co, Lead Manufacturers, Bristol, had been found in his belongings so Mr Crawford quickly penned a letter to Mr George and made sure it was dispatched on the first mail coach to Bristol.

Three days later, the letter arrived on Christopher George's desk. He had expected William to return within the next day or two from his journey and was obviously shocked by the news of this terrible tragedy. He realised that he must at once inform William's father and his fiancée.

Christopher had known William's parents for some time and had met them at various social events within the city over the years. Unfortunately, William's mother had passed away suddenly last year, and William, his father, remained in poor health. Christopher had also been at the Christmas party when William had announced his engagement to Jane, so he had met both the Mackreths and the Brights.

He thought the letter from Mr Crawford sounded hopeful, and arrangements had to be made as soon as possible. Christopher called to his Chief Clerk, "Jenkins, get me my carriage at once. Something dreadful has happened to Mr Mackreth."

"Yes, sir!" Arthur Jenkins had been with the company for many years and was well thought of, but Christian names were normally unthinkable at his level, although William sometimes called him Arthur, for which he was grateful.

The carriage arrived, and Christopher started his journey up to the Mackreth family home. Luckily, William's brothers and sister were still living at home, so William Mackreth Senior was not on his own. The journey did not take too long, although the roads to this part of the city, where most of the business community and gentry lived, were quite steep.

Christopher always felt sorry for the horses that had to pull heavy loads up these hills, but they were quite well looked after, and the Ladies of the city[5] made sure they always had plenty of water with troughs placed at strategic points. Christopher arrived at the Mackreth residence and rang the doorbell, that was swiftly answered by a housemaid.

"Is Mr Mackreth at home please? I have some urgent news for him." He handed over one of his business cards.

---

5. Wives of Bristol aldermen who were known for doing good deeds.

"Just one moment if you please, sir. I will enquire to the master."

It was but a moment when a young man arrived at the door. It was William's younger brother Henry, "Please come in, sir, please follow me. My father will see you immediately."

Henry led Christopher into the drawing room where the elderly Mr Mackreth was seated, "Please do not rise, sir," noting that the old gentleman was looking quite pale.

"It is a delight to see you, Christopher. What brings you here today? William is away, as you know."

"Yes, it is about William I have come to see you about. It is some very unpleasant news I am afraid. I came as quickly as I could."

Christopher handed over the letter to William Senior. After reading the contents, he looked even more ashen and more grave. He handed it to Henry, who quickly read it. The old man was now visibly shaking. "We must go to William and inform Jane and her family."

"Leave it with me," said Henry, who was also deeply shocked and concerned by the news. Henry was extremely close to his elder brother, as were his other siblings, George, and sister Mary, especially since their mother had passed away.

"Please allow me to take care of everything else," said Christopher. "All expenses and medical care will be paid by the company, and I will travel to Ludlow as soon as possible."

"Thank you, Christopher, for your generosity," said Henry. William was not only a much-valued friend but also had a financial interest in the Company, and Christopher George and Co had a good reputation for looking after all its employees.

Christopher then left as Henry arranged for transport to the Bright residence in Redland after making sure his father was being looked after by Bridget the housekeeper.

Chapter 6

Henry was dreading having to tell Jane. She would be devastated. He would have to stay strong for William. When he arrived at the Bright household, he was ushered through to Mr Bright in his study. John Bright was also a widower, as his wife Esther had died three years previously.

"Thank God, he is still alive!" exclaimed Jane's father as Henry explained what had befallen William. "But there is hope. He is getting the best attention. Is no one safe these days? Poor Jane! She is out shopping with her sister and should be back soon. This is going to be a terrible blow. I am sure she will want to be with William. She was so looking forward to him coming home, and they were going to make the final plans for their wedding. She's been so excited."

"I think it was a planned and callous attack, for whatever reason we do not know," said Henry. "They do have someone in custody, and we will plan to travel to Ludlow as soon as possible. But I do not think this is the right time for Jane or anyone else to visit. It is still early days, and the injuries are obviously quite horrific, according to the letter's description. I will visit you again as soon as I return. Of course, I will give you an update on William's condition."

Within about ten minutes of Henry leaving, John Bright heard the front doorbell ring, which was promptly answered by young Cassie, the housemaid. He could hear the laughter of the girls, and the door to his study burst open. "Papa," said Jane, "we have found the most wonderful material for my wedding dress."

"It's beautiful," added Mary, Jane's sister. "I have also found some lovely French material for myself and the bridesmaids."

They suddenly became aware of the sadness in their father's eyes. "Papa, whatever is the matter? What has happened?" both the girls chorused.

"I'm sorry. I have some very sad news to impart. Please sit down and listen. Something absolutely dreadful has happened to William. He was attacked where he was staying in Ludlow." Both the girls let out a cry of disbelief, Jane turned white, slipped from her chair, and collapsed to the floor.

"Quickly, get Cassie or Mrs Brooks," said Mr Bright, and Mary rushed to the door and shouted for both. Mrs Brooks ran from the kitchen where she was preparing dinner, and Cassie, who was black leading the grate in the parlour, dropped her cloth, picked up her skirts, and sped down the corridor as if her life depended on it.

"Good Lord, sir! What has happened to the Mistress?"

"We have had some terrible news about Mr Mackreth. Please get a cold compress and a little brandy," said Mr Bright, and off they scurried, soon to be back with both.

Jane was stirring, and Mary held her in her arms while Mrs Brooks held the compress to her forehead. "Papa," said Jane, "please tell me it cannot be true."

"I'm afraid it is true, my dear. Mr Christopher George received a letter today. Rest assured, though, the surgeon and doctor attending William are very hopeful, and Mr George and Henry are, as we speak, making arrangements to travel to Ludlow as soon as they can secure a stagecoach passage."

"I must go as well," said Jane through floods of tears.

"And I will go with you, of course," exclaimed Mary, also now sobbing.

"I am afraid that is not advised at this time," said Mr Bright. "William needs complete rest and is in need of constant attention."

"But Papa, we must," implored Jane.

"I'm very sorry, my dear. We must wait until Mr George and Henry return. They will then give us a report as to William's progress and when he can see visitors."

Jane was heartbroken to think of her William without her, but she understood that she must be brave and simply pray for his speedy recovery.

Chapter 7

The following day, part of the story emerged in *The Bristol Mercury* and a reporter from the paper immediately dispatched to Ludlow. Very soon, the story of this terrible event appeared in newspapers in the British Isles, America, India, and Australia.

Two days later, Christopher and Henry arrived in Ludlow and were met by Edward Cooke and Mr Crawford. They explained the whole series of events and were soon joined by Officer Hammond, who had returned to question more witnesses and conduct a thorough examination of the crime scene.

Mr Crawford reassured Henry and Christopher that William was being well cared for by his staff and making steady progress but was still weak from the great loss of blood. He advised them that they could see William, but not for too long as he did not want to overexert him.

Christopher took the opportunity to assure Mr Crawford that all costs would be covered by his company and handed him one of his business cards to forward any related accounts.

Henry had mixed emotions as they entered the bedroom. He wanted desperately to stay strong but was also afraid of seeing the severity of his brother's injuries. One of Mr Crawford's assistants had just finished washing William and helping him with his toiletry requirements.

William sat up in bed and looked at them with disbelief, followed by tears in response to seeing his brother and dear friend. Henry hugged him gently, while Christopher touched his arm lightly.

Henry could not control his tears as he gazed at the still-red fresh cut from ear to ear across his brother's mouth. He had been determined to be strong, but to no avail.

William tried to speak but could only manage an exhausted gasp. Henry spoke for him, reassuring him that everyone sent their love and best wishes for a speedy recovery. They would get him home as soon as Mr Crawford said he was fit to travel, but that surely would not be for some time.

As an excuse not to tire William further, Christopher reminded Henry that Officer Hammond was waiting for them in the Commercial Room for a full update on his findings. They were all relieved that they had caught the suspect and justice would be done.

As they had not eaten for several hours, they ordered a meal from Mr Cooke and ravenously enjoyed the porter, ham, bread, and horse radish. They waited to speak with the officer in charge, both with many unanswered questions.

Henry and Christopher were both shocked by William's appearance but gauged the optimism of Mr Crawford, Mr Hodges, and Dr Lloyd, who had all administered to William very promptly in his hour of need. They thanked God and good fortune that William had been blessed with the presence of these skilled men lodging at The Angel Inn.

Much to Mr Cooke's delight, the attack on William had significantly increased the business of the Inn, which would normally drop after the Fair. The morbid curiosity of people knew no bounds, and Mr Cooke was excited to answer questions and be the centre of attention. Drink and food sales were up, and most of his rooms were occupied, but he had the good sense to appreciate that Mr Mackreth should not be disturbed, and the police and medical gentlemen had his full attention at all times.

Officer Hammond arrived as arranged and attempted to answer all the questions put to him. Where had this villain come from? Was he a local? What was he after? Was there a motive? They both knew William carried an amount of gold in a secret compartment in his writing case, but William was known to be incredibly careful and discreet about this.

Officer Hammond answered their questions one by one as best as he could, as he also stressed that the investigation was ongoing and would be for some time. The accused had been brought to the magistrates in the guildhall the day after the attack and identified as a Josiah Mister from Birmingham, and surprisingly not from a poor family either. An officer was being sent to Birmingham on orders from the magistrates to investigate further and would report in due course. Meanwhile, the prisoner had pleaded "Not guilty," and was to be held in the local goal. Mr Baron Gurney, the magistrate, remanded Mister in custody for a further week, expecting more information from both Birmingham and the evidence from Ludlow.

Both Christopher and Henry were impressed by Officer Hammond and thought he deserved a higher rank, a surmisation that was reinforced when they met his senior, Sergeant Otley, the following morning before they left to go back to Bristol. The man reeked of porter and appeared to have grasped extraordinarily little about the case in question. A drunken imbecile, thought Henry, but kept it to himself. Henry wanted to say, "Good night," and give some words of comfort to his dear brother before he retired for the evening, before an early start back to Bristol in the morning. Both Henry and Christopher climbed the stairs to the first-floor landing and knocked gently on the door of the new room that William had been moved to. It was opened by one of the surgeon's staff who had been in attendance earlier that day.

"Can we see Mr Mackreth for a short while? We promise not to tire him."

"Of course, gentlemen," the assistant said, instantly recognising them from the morning. Otherwise, he had strict instructions from Mr Hedges and Dr Lloyd that no one was to see Mr Mackreth without their permission.

William's eyes brightened as they peered around the door. They drew up two chairs near to the bed, and William tried to speak. It was a strong word that sounded like 'glad', but then petered off.

"Don't strain yourself, dear fellow," said Christopher. "It's early days, and all will be well in due course." Henry leaned forward and gently kissed his brother on the forehead.

"Listen to Christopher. You will be well, have faith. Everything is being taken care of here and at home. We will leave tomorrow to go back to Bristol, as everyone is anxious to hear of your well-being. Jane will be so relieved to hear you are making a steady recovery, as will everyone else. We cannot wait to get you home again – but all in good time, dear brother. All in good time. Know that we all care deeply for you, William, and that you are loved dearly by us all."

The tears were beginning to well once more in everyone's eyes, and they decided to leave the room, not wishing to cause William any more distress. "Goodnight, William," Christopher said. "Be assured that we will be in contact every day to keep you aware of what's going on and hope to see you again very soon. I have the newspapers to give you as I am sure you miss *The Bristol Mercury*." A smile could be seen in William's eyes as his brother squeezed his hand before leaving the room.

Henry and Christopher boarded the early Red Rover coach the following morning and arrived in Bristol late that evening at the Bright household. They were greeted by William Mackreth Senior, his daughter Mary, Jane, her father Mr Bright, and her sister Mary, all of whom were eager to hear news of William's condition.

Henry embraced his sister and kissed her on the cheek, noting the worry on her face and the tears that had already begun to fall. "It's good news," he said, and his father breathed a sigh of relief, thanking the Lord.

Jane, on the other hand, collapsed in tears and had to be supported by her father. Upon hearing the news, she felt dizzy and almost fainted. John suggested that the men have brandy while the ladies enjoy some Bristol sherry. "Mrs Brooks, would you please see to that?" he asked. "Certainly, sir," replied Mrs Brooks, adding that she had prepared some light sandwiches for them as well.

The family had grown to rely on Mrs Brooks more than ever since the death of Jane's mother, and Mr Bright was different from some of his contemporaries in his treatment of their servants. Mrs Brooks arrived with the glasses and decanters, followed by Cassie, the housemaid, with the sandwiches.

Christopher and Henry then recounted the events of the past few days in Ludlow, including William's condition, the surgeon and doctors' reports, the police investigation, and the arrest of Mister. Everyone felt a sense of relief with Christopher's and Henry's hopefulness, but they cautioned there was a long way to go.

Although visitors were not advisable, letters would be more than welcome to hasten William's recovery. Over the next few days and months, a steady stream of letters from Jane and various family members reached William, providing him with a constant source of anticipation and sustenance.

Chapter 8

Back in Ludlow the investigation was progressing, and reports were being written for presentation to the magistrates.

A picture was beginning to form: the blood trail from rooms 17 to 20; the blood on the curtains in the accused's room; the pot containing water which tasted of alum; a wrapped block of alum found in Josiah Mister's belongings; and the razor found in the Baker's Yard next door, in line of sight with the bedroom window of the accused.

As far as Sergeant Otley and Officer Hammond were concerned, it was all coming together, and they were just waiting for the report from Birmingham. As usual, Sergeant Otley was taking all the glory, while Officer Hammond did all the donkey work.

The following day, while retracing his steps and reviewing his findings in room 17, Officer Hammond sat down on the chair to study his notes and make some further scribbles. His pencil fell to the floor, so he reached down to retrieve it. Today, the room was well-lit by sunlight, whereas the days preceding were dark and overcast. The sun clearly revealed thick dust on the floor, but as the Officer lifted his head, he caught a glimpse of where, just under the bed, the dust had been disturbed. He could now distinctly make out the shape of a what could be the rough outline of a figure.

He decided to take a closer look, and on moving the bed, he also found a piece of sandpaper[6] and a spent Lucifer match. Edward Cooke certainly did not keep much of an eye on the cleaning of the

---

6. Sandpaper would be used if you did not have a lucifer striking box that was often silver with have a serrated area on its side.

rooms, he thought. Luckily, the inn's slovenly approach to tidiness had just given him a valuable clue. This is where the assailant had obviously hidden. And the match? It was then he remembered reading one of the other officers' reports on when Mister entered the town. He had spoken to two youngsters who had been teasing a wasp nest. According to the boys, Mister had stopped to watch and said, "You need one of these," pulling a Lucifer match from his waistcoat pocket. But as the Red Rover mail coach arrived, he had replaced the match as quickly as he had presented it and walked away at a fast pace towards the approaching coach that was headed to The Angel.

Two days later, Josiah Mister was brought to the Ludlow Guildhall by the gaoler and presented to Mr Downes, the Magistrate's Clerk, the Mayor, and Mr J. Hutchings, who presided. Mister was wearing the same clothes he was arrested in, and he was observed as being calm and nonchalant at the proceedings.

Mr Crawford and Mr Hodges who were also in attendance were asked about William's well-being. "The gentleman is in no fit condition to come to court at this time," confirmed Mr Crawford. It was suggested by Mr Downes that the evidence be taken in the large dining room at the Angel Inn at 10 o'clock in the morning in one week's time when Mr Mackreth would hopefully be well enough to attend. Mr Hutchings asked for this to be noted, and the magistrate's clerk recorded it. The prisoner was then led back to his cell by the gaoler. It was also hoped that the inquiries in Birmingham would be concluded by then.

The following week, as arranged, the magistrates, along with four official persons and some ladies, assembled at the Angel Inn. The prisoner was brought in by the gaoler and seemed flustered on his first appearance, but he immediately regained his composure. A few minutes later, Mr Downes, the Magistrates Clerk, entered the room followed by William Mackreth, whose appearance sparked a pained interest in all those present. William bowed to the magistrates upon entering and was conducted to a seat opposite the prisoner, who surveyed him with anxious attention.

William still felt quite weak but assured Mr Crawford, after a concerned look, that he would manage. "I will request a stop to the proceedings if I feel you shouldn't go on," said Mr Crawford, who had formed a close bond over the previous weeks with William, both as a patient and as a friend.

William, who had always been regarded as a young man of handsome appearance, was still attractive despite his injuries. His modest and retiring manner had raised a strong feeling in his favour, and he was regarded with much attention by everyone in the town. The wound in his face had caused a horrid furrow to be visible, reaching from one ear to the other, across the mouth, and dividing the face into two parts, eliciting a great amount of sympathy for the young accountant who had suffered such an injustice. The wound had started to heal far better than anyone would have expected and would continue to do so, but the scar would never be completely effaced.

The mayor, together with Mr J Hutching and William Harding Esqs managed the proceedings with several county magistrates, including Sir W R Boughton, also present. All paid the utmost attention to William's statement as he explained what had happened on the night in question. He gave his name, William Miller Mackreth, and said, "I am a traveller and business partner of lead shot manufacturer Christopher George and Co of Bristol. I arrived in Ludlow at the Angel Inn on Wednesday, the 19th of August, arriving at between five and six 'clock in the evening. I was shown to my room and my luggage was brought up by the porter.

I left the Inn and called to see several persons that we do business with and was later joined back at the Angel later that evening by a Mr Bradford, another business colleague. We were in the Commercial Room for about an hour, and during that time, several gentlemen came in, but I do not know who they were. Mr Bradford left, and I continued to write in my notebook. Several other gentlemen came in, but I took no notice as to who they were. It was getting quite late, so I closed my driving-box[7] and requested a chambermaid show me to my room. My shoes were taken for cleaning by the boot boy, and I was given a pair of slippers and guided to my sleeping quarters. I went to my bed and slept well until I was awoken in the early hours by a sharp sensation on my neck.

Struggling out of bed, I felt someone push past me. I smashed my bedroom window and tried to shout for help and fire to attract attention. As I put my hand to my mouth, I realised the extent of my injuries. I went to my door, which was open several inches, and stepped onto the landing. I turned to go down the stairs, but I remember thinking I had locked my door as I had £90 in gold and notes in my driving-box, which I wanted to keep safe."

"Thank you, Mr Mackreth. Please be seated," said Mr Downes.

The chambermaid Nellie Winters was then called to confirm her written statement. In particular, Mr Downes asked if there was anything she remembered that she may have overlooked in her original account.

"Well, sir," said Nellie, "I recall there was some light showing from room number 20, which would not have been seen if the door had been tightly closed. Also, when I was allowed to clean the room by Officer Hammond, I noticed the candle had burned down to its end. When I thought more about it, I thought it very unusual as it must have been burning for a very long time."

"Thank you, Miss," said Mr Downes and Nellie was permitted to leave the room.

Officer Hammond stood up, and Mr Downes motioned for him to speak. "If I may say so, sir, I have tried the door in darkness with a lighted candle in the room and can confirm that no light can be seen on the landing with the door firmly closed, only when it is slightly open and not secure."

---

7. A wooden box lockable box for writing paper, pens, ink often with a secret compartment for holding valuables.

"Thank you, Officer Hammond. That is most interesting," said Mr Downes, carefully making notes amidst the mutterings of the magistrates and other officials.

He then turned to the prisoner, Josiah Mister. "Do you wish to ask Mr Mackreth any questions?"

"Yes," said Mister, looking confidently at William. "Do you know me, sir?"

"I do not," said William, "but there is a familiarity about you, as I have previously stated."

Mister turned to Mr Downes and the magistrates, and with an arrogant air, clearly proclaimed, "I could not have done the crime I am accused of. The door was not forced, as the Officer's evidence stated, and I remained in my room. I am not guilty!" Mister looked directly at William with his little staring, snake-like eyes, and a slight smirk to his thin lips.

In an effort to diffuse Mister's outburst, Mr Downes announced, "I have received news from Birmingham and Shrewsbury. The Officer investigating there should arrive in Ludlow within the next couple of days. I therefore suggest we adjourn until one week today and continue at The Guildhall at 10 o'clock in the morning on that day. The prisoner will be held in custody until that time."

Mister was led away and had to be protected from the hostile waiting crowd that had gathered in the street outside.

Mr Downes thanked William and hoped the morning proceedings had not been too stressful and that he would continue to gain good health. William bowed to the magistrates and left the room with Mr Crawford.

Chapter 9

The attempted murder in Ludlow was now being avidly followed by every paper in the country and as far as India with the larger newspapers sending journalists directly to the Shropshire town, and their proprietors then selling their record of events to the smaller regional publications.

William was receiving regular letters from his beloved Jane, as well as from his father, brothers, and sisters, updating him on the immense interest the outside world had taken in the horrendous attack on him. He was also receiving a large number of letters of support from people he had never met before. Some of his fans were quite passionate, which touched and amused William in equal measure.

"Love and Best Wishes" for a speedy recovery were in abundance, and he no longer felt the despair and loneliness that had engulfed him after the shock of the attack had subsided. The people of Ludlow had shown great kindness and care towards him, something that he would never forget. William continued to pray for the day he could return home to his Jane, family, and friends, but it would still be some time yet.

William read all the papers that were brought to him and in particular felt well enough to reply to a report he had read in the *Ludlow Globe*, which was duly printed by the paper a week later. It said, "A private letter was received yesterday from the gentleman Mr William Miller Mackreth in response to our reporting the terrible attack on his person at the Angel Inn....*Sir, I am happy to tell you that the neck wound is now nearly closed and would likely be fully healed in a couple of days.* He goes on to say that his face was thoroughly healed, and the union had taken place throughout the inside within 24 hours after the cheeks were de-severed. The surface of his tongue had been cut off as the weapon drew through his mouth but was now quite healed. He also addressed a portion of the evidence that read very strangely but was of easy explanation. The cook stated that when she entered the room, he was shaking his clenched fist at her master, which was quite true, but it was the most expressive mode of denial he could give the landlord when he said to him, "Good God, whatever made you do it!" For, at the time, he did not have the power of utterance. William also clarified that the statement in some papers that he was taking solid food was incorrect; he was still sustained by liquids until the throat wound closed, a portion of which escaped through the wound as he swallowed. The continuation cut on both sides was now perfectly united.

The hearing resumed in a week or so and William was picked up by a fly carriage and taken to the Guildhall, where large crowds had gathered to see William and Josiah Mister arrive. There was quite a large police presence as hostilities were expected. It was noticeable that a large part of the crowd were ladies and women of the town, some say due to word getting around of how handsome William was despite his injuries.

Many had arrived early to secure a seat in the Guildhall, which had a limited capacity, and the interest was far greater than the seating arrangements allowed. William had arrived before Mister, but the boos and 'Hang him' chants could be heard quite clearly inside the building. A scuffle broke out when a handcuffed Mister finally arrived with the gaoler.

Mr Downes, the magistrates' clerk, together with the mayor, Sir W R Boughton, and the magistrates were already seated. William was shown to his seat by Mr Downes, and there was a subdued chatter across the courtroom, and an abundance of smiles from the fairer sex, which, despite his love for Jane, William could not help but find both comforting and flattering.

New evidence had been produced since the last court appearance. A pair of white bloodied stockings wrapped in an old newspaper had been found in a woodpile in the stable yard. The newspaper was dated a couple of weeks before the attack on William. In addition, the Officer had returned from Birmingham with a report on his findings.

Mister had denied that the razor found in the yard outside his window was his and that his last shave before his arrest was at a barber in Shrewsbury. Investigations in Shrewsbury proved negative after an officer had visited every barber in the town. No one recognised his description from the artist drawings presented to them. The officer also visited Mister's lodgings in Birmingham, which he shared with a Mr Edwin Thatcher, who stated that he had lent Josiah a razor that was unset.[8] He had not had the razor back and assumed Josiah had taken it with him on his journey.

The magistrates consulted together. They had listened to all the witnesses and had already taken all the statements into account. The mayor stood up and addressed the prisoner, "Josiah Mister, we have now brought this investigation to a conclusion, and it is my duty to tell you that, after having given your case every consideration – after attending patiently to every word muttered by the numerous witnesses brought against you, and our examination of these – we consider that there is beyond doubt sufficient evidence against you to warrant us to send you to trial at the next Shrewsbury assizes, for an attempt to take away the life of Mr Mackreth, at the Angel Inn, Ludlow, by cutting his throat with a razor. You therefore stand committed for trial, and the gaoler will hold you in safe custody until you are moved to Shrewsbury jail."

The prisoner looked shaken for a second or two but then appeared to receive the summation with great indifference and immediately

---

8. A set razor is highly sharpened, ready for shaving, whereas an unset razor is unsharpened.

sat down in the dock, where he was handcuffed once again and led away.

William felt and looked relieved, and there was a loud cheer from the public gallery, followed by another cheer from the waiting crowd outside as soon as they heard the news that Mister would go to trial.

Mr Downes, the magistrates' clerk, came across to William, Officer Hammond, and his now friend Mr Crawford.

"I doubt very much if the trial will start until next spring, knowing how busy Shrewsbury assizes are," said Mr Downes. " I expect you will be glad to be able to return home, William."

"I most certainly will," said William.

"Everyone will be notified if their presence will be required in Shrewsbury. Gentlemen, good day to you and safe journeys."

The fly was waiting to transport him and Mr Crawford back to The Angel, where a crowd had gathered. The landlord, Mr Cooke, was waiting for them. "Come this way, gentlemen. I expect you need some refreshment," he said, heading towards The Commercial Room where cold meats and porter were laid out for them.

"I cannot thank you enough, Robert," William said. It was only the second time William had called Mr Crawford by his first name, although he had addressed William by his first name from the beginning. "I owe my life to you, and I shall be eternally grateful."

"That's simply my profession, William. I am only glad that I was in the right place at the right time, and do not forget I had help from my colleagues, Mr Hedges and Dr Lloyd. And now, I also have a new and dear friend," said Mr Crawford. They both rose from the table and shook hands.

"I will thank everyone before I leave and will write to you before I next come to Ludlow so we can arrange to meet, as I will surely return when things are back to normal. And, of course, we still have the trial next year."

Mr Crawford nodded, "Do exactly as I have told you William to continue your recovery and have a safe journey until we meet again."

When William returned to his room, he found several notes from well-wishers, and several large bunches of flowers that had been put on the dresser from people in the town. He was quite overwhelmed, and it restored his faith that there was certainly more love and kindness in the world than evil.

Chapter 10

It was now autumn, and William had been away from Jane and his family for many weeks. He was both excited and terrified at the prospect of meeting them all again. Would Jane still want and love him with his change in appearance? Not only had Mr Crawford and his team saved William's life, but they had also done a wonderful job on his appearance with their skills and care. He could visibly see the improvements in his scars, almost on a daily basis, but he would never be or feel quite the same. He felt fine in his health, but a cloud of doubt crept in when he was on his own and had time to think. With the accounts paid, he would catch the Red Rover back to Bristol as soon as possible and had sent a letter by an earlier mail coach, hoping it would reach Jane and his family before he did. He would face whatever there was to come. After all, he was still alive and remained optimistic for the future.

The next morning William made his way down to the Commercial Room and met Mr Cooke. "Morning, sir. Is there anything I can get you?"

"No, thank you, Mr Cooke," said William. "But tell me, are there still seats available on the next Red Rover?"

"They are terribly busy today, sir, looking at the number of passengers waiting outside. You will have to go to the booking agents in Broad Street to see what the situation is. Mr Vickers did mention, when he was in the other evening and asking about your well-being, that the company would credit your return ticket to Bristol under the circumstances."

"That would be exceedingly good of them," said William, and he headed out to Broad Street.

He was greeted almost immediately by passersby and tradesmen coming out of their shops as the word went around. Folks were pointing and nudging each other in an excited manner, "There's that poor Mr Mackreth," Mavis, a young girl from the bakers, was heard saying. "How handsome he still is! I wouldn't kick him out of my bed!"

"Shame on you," said her sister. "You're wicked."

"Well, I wouldn't," retorted Mavis.

When William arrived at the booking agent, Mr Vickers recognised him straight away. "Come in, sir, and take a chair. It's good to see you in such good health after such a hideous ordeal."

"I am feeling much recovered," said William. "And wish to return home as soon as possible, please."

"Of course, sir. We will do our very best for you, but tomorrow will be the earliest, I am afraid, due to the demand for Birmingham, and, of course, there will be no charge and the full reimbursement on your earlier return ticket."

"I thank you, sir," said William. "That is most civil and courteous of you."

On his return to the Inn, Nellie Winters came scurrying over to him. "You have a visitor off The Rover, sir. He is in the Commercial Room," as she pointed towards the door.

There, rising from his seat, was another good-looking young man. I wonder if he will be staying the night, thought Nellie to herself. Might be worth maybe a few shillings or even half a sovereign, she mused.

William could not believe his eyes. "Dear brother! What on earth are you doing here?" he cried, hugging Henry.

"I received your letter and got the very first stage from Bristol. We could not let you travel back alone. Everyone is so happy to see you again, and Jane wanted to come with me, but we assured her you would be home soon. She is so desperate to see you."

Henry stood back to get a good look at his brother. "William, it's still you. You have a slight scar, but it is nothing. You look so well. It's a miracle."

Henry rang the service bell and ordered two large brandies to celebrate. They had so much to talk about.

William explained that he would have to come up to Shrewsbury sometime next year for the trial, but that was still some way off. He was now as desperate as Jane to be back in Bristol and reunited with everyone he loved.

They both slept well that night and woke up refreshed, ready for the early coach that morning. The landlord, Edward Cooke and his staff wished them both a safe journey.

At the same time Josiah Mister was being transported in irons by the mail coach to the county prison in Shrewsbury, in the custody of Mr Davies, the Ludlow gaoler. Fellow passengers directed looks of great disdain towards him, trying to keep as far away from him as possible. However, there was one exception, a young lady who had sent him a new shirt while he was in prison.

Mister appeared quite indifferent to everyone, and as they eventually passed the Unicorn Inn where he had originally followed Mr Ludlow, he looked the other way until they arrived at the Sun Tavern, where a fly was waiting to take him to the prison. Several hundred people had assembled there, anxious to get a glimpse of the prisoner. As Mister entered the huge gates, there was a roar of hisses and boos.

The trip back to Bristol was comfortable, apart from the odd stare from one or two passengers. Whenever peoples' looks lingered on him, William began to think about Jane. He was no longer the man he was when he left her. He knew the scars on his face would never completely disappear, although the surgeons had told him the healing of his facial wounds had been quite remarkable. William remained unsure whether Jane would still want him and accept his new appearance. Would it be honourable and fair to expect her to stand by her promise to marry him? He turned these thoughts over and over in his head, feeling the anxiety in his stomach churning and wrenching with the thought of losing the love of his life.

The conversation in the coach helped to distract him slightly, but time still passed slowly as passengers left and joined the coach at the various stops along the way. William remained in a daze, and the chatter passed over him as he could not concentrate on listening to others. There was just too much turmoil and noise going through his own mind. Henry noticed that his brother was not his usual self but said nothing. He did not want to stir up bad memories for him and assured himself that his brother would return to his old character in due course.

In contrast, Henry engaged happily with the various businessmen, tradespeople, and gentlemen who made up the mix of passengers. Conversation flowed, bringing their home city of Bristol closer and closer. Henry soon recognised the countryside on the approach to the city, first passing Thornbury, then Filton, and onto the main road into the centre from the north.

The city was as busy as ever, and they soon arrived at the central post office. Their luggage was unloaded, and Henry went to get a cab from a nearby rank of assorted horse-drawn vehicles, which always tried to get a spot when the mail coach arrived, as it meant good business and a tip if they were lucky.

A smart young man driving a hansom cab caught Henry's eye, and he hired him immediately to take them to the Bright residence in Redland. The cab driver deftly manoeuvred the cab into position, jumping down and saluting William as he did so. The young man named Isaac had always been told by his father that "Courtesy Costs Nothing." He was polite and respectful to all, and he was treated the same in return. His father had built up the business from nothing and now owned two cabs with nothing owed to money lenders or anyone else, a fact of which he was enormously proud.

Isaac opened the cab door, and William and Henry ascended. He packed up their luggage, and they were on their way. Within half an hour or so, they were at the Bright residence. William felt a slight emptiness in his stomach and a sense of trepidation, not from seeing his family, but the thought of seeing Jane again after so long.

How would she react when she saw him? The door was opened by Mrs Brooks, the housekeeper, who took one look at William and embraced him in her ample arms.

"Oh, sir! It's so wonderful to see you. God bless you," she exclaimed. The entire family rushed into the hallway to greet him, and within seconds, Jane was in his arms with tears streaming down her face. "My Darling, you are home at last. I have missed you so much…" Jane's voice began to tremble, "I thought … I thought I may never see you again."

William had the love of his life in his arms again. He felt her warmth and her wonderful smell that he never forgotten all the time he was confined in Ludlow. He felt the same passion as when he first met her. When everything had been so uncertain, William knew exactly what he wanted, and she was standing right in front of him.

Chapter 11

His gaze continued to fix on Jane who was seated on the sofa with her family. William's siblings, George, and Mary were also present, along with their father and Henry. The sitting room was packed with relatives, including Jane's father, sister Mary, younger sister Eleanor and brother Joseph. Eleanor was married to Humphrey, who was in the shipping business, and Joseph, William's other brother was training to be an accountant and lived above the company office in the city. Mary, the youngest sibling, had been tutored since their mother's passing and now lived with her Aunt Clarissa in Westbury-on-Trym. Clarissa was a widow and an academic who ran a day school from her large house. She believed in educating young ladies in languages, maths, manners, and good English, emphasising that they should not just be ornamental but should have more to offer than producing sons and heirs. Mary was the exception as she lived in and got along very well with her aunt. She found learning enjoyable and looked forward to being home with the family occasionally.

As emotions ran high and everyone celebrated William's return, Mrs Brooks took young Cassie to one side and asked her to pay the cab driver the fare that Henry had given her. Henry would usually do it himself, but the family occasion had been too overwhelming for protocol on this occasion. Isaac had brought the luggage into the outer hallway and was patiently waiting when Cassie arrived to hand him the fare with a generous tip. Isaac smiled and thanked her, and Cassie felt herself blush.

"What might your name be my pretty one?" asked Isaac.

"Don't be so cheeky and mind your own business…but it happens to be Cassie if you want to know." With a wide grin on her face.

"How would you like to walk out with me on your day off?"

Cassie felt flustered. She had never been out with a boy alone before. What would Mrs Brooks say? They arranged to meet on Sunday afternoon, her only day off, and Isaac promised to pick her up on the corner at 1 o'clock.

When Cassie returned, Mrs Brooks noted her delay with a knowing look and reminded her to take refreshments to the family. As Isaac turned the carriage around to return to the city, Henry called out to him and requested two carriages to pick them up at 9 o'clock that evening to return to Clifton. Isaac agreed, happy to have another job, and he secretly hoped he might see Cassie again when he returned.

Upon arriving home at Hanover Place, his father was watering the horses and Isaac excitedly informed his father of the additional job that evening. His father was pleased and asked what else was making him so happy. Isaac could not contain his smile as he told his father about the pretty girl he had met in service at the house.

"Just go steady and respect her, you hear?" said his father, Joseph.

"Yes, Da, of course, I will," replied Isaac.

Joseph knew he could not wish for a better son. His mother would have been proud if she had seen the fine young man he had grown up to be. Sadly, his beloved wife Rachael had been taken by the cholera which had swept through inner Bristol and some of the posher areas some years earlier.

In the mid-19th century, Bristol had the worst water supply in all of England and could not cope with the amount of sewage produced. Most of it went straight into the River Frome, or the River Avon, which was used by the poor for drinking water. The water was not boiled, so disease was rife amongst the lower classes who could not afford the penny a day for drinkable water. Sewage seeped into springs everywhere, and even upper-class areas like Clifton were not immune from time to time. To contain the epidemic, pump handles were removed from drinking supplies to stop its use in various parts of the city. Graveyards were full, and bodies exposed to scavenging animals, all adding to a putrid stench and yet more deaths. The Council acted, and Arnos Vale Cemetery was opened in 1837 to help solve the problem ... and make a profit.

"We must make sure the carriages are clean and in good order for this evening," said Joseph. Much of their trade was repeat business built up over the years, enabling him to eventually become his own boss after being apprenticed to old Charlie Briffet as a young lad of 12 years of age. Charlie had taught him the ropes, and this is what he was now passing on to Isaac.

At around a quarter to nine, Isaac felt a little jump in his heart as they set off back to Redland, desperately hoping that Cassie would answer the door when they arrived.

Ever punctual, they arrived in Redland just before nine in the evening as requested. Isaac rang the doorbell and held his breath. Seconds seemed like long minutes, and Cassie answered. She blushed again, and in turn Isaac's face reddened.

"Good evening, sir," said Cassie slightly embarrassed. "I will inform the master that the carriages are here."

"Don't forget Sunday," whispered Isaac.

"I might," teased Cassie, knowing full well she would not. She had never felt so excited in all her life at the prospect of courting a young man.

Mrs Brooks had purposely allowed Cassie to answer the door on this occasion, something that would normally be her duty. She was not as hard-hearted as she sometimes appeared, and she had become very fond of this young girl in her care.

Mrs Brooks announced that the coaches had arrived, and William, his father, brothers Henry and George, and Sister Mary left for their home in Clifton.

Chapter 12

William arranged to meet with Jane and her father in a few days' time to discuss the marriage arrangements, as they had decided to make plans as soon as possible. Apart from the traditional financial costs, family and friend invitations, bridesmaids, and duties of all concerned, there was plenty to discuss.

William arrived at the Bright residence and was warmly greeted by Jane and her younger sister, who were clearly excited to see him. "I have missed you," said Jane, promptly giving William a kiss on his cheek, followed by a kiss on the other cheek by her younger sister, Mary.

"Father's waiting," said Jane, and William's stomach filled with butterflies as they entered the parlour. "Come in, dear boy," said Mr Bright, as cheerful as ever, and William knew he need not have worried.

Jane had already decided on a wedding dress, which was being hand-made by Madame Du Pont in Bristol. Fittings were well under way, and the bridesmaids had been selected, with their gowns' designs chosen to complement the bride. Mary would be the chief bridesmaid, together with her younger sister Eleanor, and William's younger sister Mary. Tradition normally dictated that William's elder brother George would be best man, but he would be away on business so Henry would do the honours with Joseph as one of the ushers. The wedding would take place at St. Paul's Church, Bristol.

William and John stepped out into the well-tended garden to discuss the more serious side of the betrothal. John knew that William had a good income from his business partnership and other interests, and he also knew that he was a man of good reputation and honesty, as he had made it his business to find out in the city. He knew his beloved daughter would be cherished and looked after, but the question that was most uppermost on his mind was where they would live.

He put this question to William, who explained that his brother Henry had been looking into some eligible properties and had already come up with a number of properties for sale, the most suitable so far being at Kingsdown in an area called Montague Hill. According to William, it had five family bedrooms and servants' quarters in the attic and its own water supply. The price was fair, and William had already made an offer to be negotiated by his solicitors. If all went well, the house would be ready before the wedding.

As was the etiquette of the day, property was typically a man's choice, yet William had consulted Jane on the matter, and she completely trusted his judgment.

Mr Bright felt happy about his daughter's future with this young man, and now that everything was settled, the two of them returned to the house for the tea that Mrs Brooks had prepared for them all.

Jane's Great-Aunt Charlotte and Uncle Charles had kindly offered to hold a reception in their large house in Queen's Square in the centre of Bristol as a wedding gift. Great-Aunt Charlotte was well-known for her extravagant parties, so it was sure to be a grand affair. Although Jane's Great Aunt and Uncle were exceptionally successful and wealthy, they held no airs or graces. Carriages had been arranged for everyone on the special day, although some of the richer family members owned their own private carriages and employed grooms.

William had quickly re-established himself in the lead business with his dear friend and colleague Christopher George, who would be an honoured guest at the wedding. William found himself a subject of curiosity among their customers, and strangely, wives would also be in attendance, hoping to catch a glimpse of William, who had become a minor celebrity due to the news coverage.

Although he had become used to the attention, it was a constant reminder of what had happened, which was never far from his waking thoughts and dreams. William reminded himself daily how grateful he was to be alive and soon to be married to the woman he loved.

Back at the Bright household, everyone was busy with the wedding arrangements, and according to the solicitors, Kingsdown House was going ahead at a pace. Once finalised, Jane would have to interview for a housekeeper and maid with the help of Mrs Brooks. William had decided to leave it all to Jane. She felt proud of the trust he had placed in her, especially as this was normally the prerogative of the male family members. William often surprised her with his unconventional manners, and his ordeal had taught her that he had a strength of character and independence that was not constrained by Victorian values.

The kitchen was busy as usual, with Mrs Brooks and Cassie taking it all in their stride. Tradespeople were calling, and extra provisions were being ordered. "Do you think we will be invited to the wedding?" asked Cassie.

"Good grief, girl! Whoever do you think you are?" exclaimed Mrs Brooks, not really believing what she was hearing. "Don't get above your station, my girl. Whatever goes on in that mind of yours, I do not know. Ever since you went courting with that young Isaac, you have not been the same, your head in the clouds. Just remember your place, young lady, and don't you ever bring any disgrace to this house, do you hear? The family has been very good to you. Now get on with your work."

"Yes, Mrs Brooks," said Cassie sheepishly, not wanting to upset her any further. She had had a wonderful afternoon with Isaac, though, and the memory came flooding back. She could not wait to see him again next Sunday afternoon.

As the big day drew closer, the rings arrived from the bespoke jewellers and were given to Henry to take care of. He felt very honoured but also a bit nervous, so he made sure they went into his father's safe for safe keeping.

Jane, the two Marys, and Eleanor were all having fittings for their dresses, together with the other bridesmaids and little flower girls who were all cousins of Jane. There was so much anticipation in the air that the excited flower girls had to be scolded from time to time, which usually brought forward a few temporary tears.

Every time Mrs Brooks saw Jane in her dress for fitting with Madame Du Pont, she was filled with emotion. Memories of her own wedding to her dear Albert, who had passed away many years ago during a further cholera epidemic of 1832 that struck Bristol, came flooding back. Though they were happily married, they were never blessed with children, so she now looked upon Jane as the child she never had. Jane had been a young child when she joined the Bright household, and Mrs Brooks had seen her grow up to become a fine woman. They had spent many hours in the kitchen together, with Jane always curious and continually asking questions, wanting to help with baking or cooking. The Bright household was now her family, and she did not want anything else. They did not treat her like a servant, and she was always respected and shown great kindness.

Tomorrow was the rehearsal day at St. Paul's in Portland Square, and Jane was looking forward to seeing William again. He was now back at his business, and she did not see him quite as often as she would like. But no matter, she was consoled by the thought that they would soon be together forever as husband and wife.

Ten days had passed, with all the arrangements and mini panics by various members of the families taking place. A truly kind offer of a honeymoon venue had been given by one of Jane's relatives, who had a large house in Ottery St Mary in Devon. They would be away for several months in Portugal on business, and the house would be fully staffed and at their disposal.

Chapter 13

It was late September when the morning of William and Jane's wedding finally arrived, and everyone in both the Mackreth and Bright households was up early. Tradespeople were arriving at the Bright residence, and Madame Du Pont and her assistants had arrived with all the dresses. The bridesmaids and flower girls were all having their final fitting just in case, and it was chaos in the ladies' bedrooms. Mrs Brooks and Cassie were up at half past five in the morning make sure everyone had early breakfasts and refreshments ready for later.

The Mackreth household was equally busy. Bridget, the housekeeper, and Florence, the housemaid, had been up since dawn to prepare breakfasts, do last-minute ironing, and clean boots. As best man, Henry was awaiting the arrival of the barber to give all the men of the household an expert shave and trim. He had already fetched the rings from his father's safe and checked them for the tenth time, discussing the whole procedure with William once again.

Ten days prior, a wedding rehearsal had been held at St. Paul's, not as grand as St. Mary Redcliffe, which was closer to Queen's Square and was the preferred venue for most of the family. Yet it remained William and Jane's choice and they felt more comfortable with a simpler venue.

"Henry, for goodness' sake, everything will be fine!" in response to his brother's wittering. On the outside, William seemed quite calm and in full control, but inside, his stomach was turning over and over. To overcome his anxiety, he turned his thoughts to his beloved Jane and their first night together. There was a knock on the bedroom door, and Florence announced that the barber had arrived.

"Thank you, Florence. We will be right there," said Henry. Once the barber had left, Henry formally addressed his brothers. "Gentlemen, we must leave no later than quarter past eleven, so I would suggest we all finish dressing as soon as possible and meet up in the library for a toast before we leave for the church." Henry was taking his responsibilities very seriously, and the family had noticed quite a mature change in him. William Snr was already in the library when his sons, now dressed in their new wedding attire, looked every inch the gentlemen that Mr Mackreth and his late wife had brought them up to be.

Mr Mackreth asked Bridget to bring in a special bottle of Scottish whisky that he had been keeping for such an occasion. A bottle of single malt 'Long John' from the Lochy Bridge Fort William distillery, not too far from where the Mackreth/Macrae Clan originated from. The drinks were poured, and William and Jane's health and future prosperity were toasted.

An hour later, William's carriage pulled into Portland Square. There was already at least a dozen or so carriages there, including a couple of the new Clarences[9] and landaus owned by the wealthier members of the families. The event was creating quite an attraction as announcements had been made in all the newspapers. Not only were the Mackreths a highly regarded Bristol name, but Jane was also from the prominent Bright dynasty, which had commercial interests in Brunel's SS *Great Britain*, the Gibbs guano and wine empire, and many more famous enterprises of the day.

---

9. A Clarence carriage was popular in the early 19th century. Named after the Duke of Clarence who later became King William IV, it was a closed, four-wheeled horse-drawn vehicle with a projecting glass front and seats for four passengers inside. A Landau was a four-wheeled luxury carriage with a roof that could be let down.

As they entered the church, they recognised and greeted many friends and family in their finery. Jane's brother Joseph was already seated on the side reserved for the bride's family, as William and Henry made their way to the front on the opposite side. William noticed and acknowledged his dear friend and business associate Christopher George and his charming wife Elizabeth as they proceeded up the aisle.

As William stood with his best man, he started to feel a little light-headed, and again his stomach began to churn. He wanted to sit down and looked at his brother, who was checking for the eleventh time that he still had the ring. Henry noticed his brother, who always had a healthy complexion, looking a little pale. "What's the matter, William? Are you not feeling well?"

"I am sure I will feel better if I can sit down for a minute or so," said William. Henry held his arm as William sat down. "I think it must be nerves," added William. "With everything that has happened, I can hardly believe this day has arrived."

The Reverend James Fouracres appeared in front of the couple with his usual cheery and reassuring smile. He could not help but think of the fee and collection that would result from such a wealthy congregation. Meanwhile, the organ played to herald the arrival of the bride. The procession was led by Jane and her father, followed by the retinue of maids of honour, bridesmaids, and flower girls. William was struck by how beautiful Jane looked in the hazy light from the large church window. It was a dream-like picture that would stay with him for the rest of his life.

As they both took a small step forward towards the Reverend Fouracres, Jane glanced shyly at William, thinking about how handsome he looked. She was anxious and shaking and just wanted to hear the words "husband and wife." The giving of the bride, vows, and exchange of rings were over in seconds, before they and their fathers were putting their signatures to the wedding certificate and church records.

As William and Jane almost skipped back down the aisle, there was a throng of people outside St Paul's. Loud cheers erupted as hundreds of rose petals cascaded down, and everyone wanted to shake their hands and wish them luck. Henry cleared a pathway to the waiting open coach, and they both sat there as they were being showered with yet more rose petals and shouts of good wishes. The rest of their families and friends followed, and they were soon off in a grand procession of carriages to Queen's Square and the wedding reception that awaited them.

Upon their arrival, staff were waiting for them, and they were offered glasses of champagne as they entered the grand hallway. The couple were guided to a room aside for the wedding breakfast, which had been opened via large double doors to the adjacent room to accommodate the considerable number of guests. Great-Aunt Charlotte and Uncle Charles were in the Clarence Carriage behind them, followed by both fathers, maids of honour, and bridesmaids. Over the next hour, the three hundred and 50 guests were introduced to the new Mr and Mrs William Mackreth while the servants handed out champagne and canapés.

As the last guests passed on their congratulations, Great-Aunt Charlotte came over and whispered in Jane's ear, "Jane dear, let my maid Rosemary show you to your rooms as I expect you would like to refresh yourselves before the Reception Dinner and have a little rest. Just come down when you are ready, but everyone will be called at half past five for dinner at six."

"Thank you, dear Aunt Charlotte, it is all so wonderful, and you are so kind," Jane replied.

"Nonsense, dear. Now you and William follow Rosemary to your rooms," suggested Great-Aunt Charlotte. William finally managed to slip away from the well-wishers to join his bride. He gently reached for Great-Aunt Charlotte's hand and whispered, "Thank you for everything." Great-Aunt Charlotte felt a slight blush of embarrassment to her cheeks as Rosemary led them away.

Great-Aunt Charlotte and Uncle Charles had given William and Jane a suite of rooms overlooking the square, complete with their own bathroom and a modern style toilet. "Anything you require, sir, just pull the bell," said Rosemary as she curtsied and left the room.

Some people have all the luck, she thought to herself. But then again, she was lucky herself to be in such a position in a grand household. It was something she had worked hard for, to become the mistress's personal maid. It gave her position and privilege under Mr Angus McGill, the head butler, who oversaw the under butler, the footmen, and most of the servants. Unofficially, she was on a par with Mrs Robertson, the housekeeper. She could not complain.

Although Rosemary was not educated conventionally, she was not stupid and had her wits about her. She had learned fast in the school of life and took advantage of opportunities. Rosemary came from an extremely poor household in the St Phillips area of Bristol, with six siblings in a two-up, two-down terraced house. Her father worked hard in a local tannery, but there was never enough money to feed or clothe the family he loved. He and his wife Mabel had met and married at 18 and had given birth to their first child within a year. And so, it continued in a life of poverty with an ever-increasing number of mouths to feed. There would have been more, but diseases and miscarriages took their toll. Rosemary, at the age of 23, made sure it did not happen to her. Love, she decided, did not put bread on the table. Rosemary was petite and pretty and had her share of attention from young men, but she resisted what she thought of as an emotional trap.

Unaware of William's recent past, as she was unable to read, Rosemary felt more envy than compassion for the newlyweds, who had waited so long for this moment alone.

Chapter 14

As Rosemary closed the door, William and Jane could wait no longer. They flew into each other's arms and felt their combined passions flow. "My darling, you don't know how many times I've thought about this moment. You look so beautiful," he whispered as he kissed Jane gently on her lips and felt her respond to the closeness of his body.

"I want you so much too, William, but we must wait a little longer, my love," said Jane in a whisper as the strength seemed to drain from her whole body. "I love you so much."

"I love you too, my darling," said William, "from the moment I first saw you."

"Aunt Charlotte and Uncle Charles told me that they will be leaving for their house in Leigh Woods this evening," said Jane. "So, we will be here alone except for the servants. Let's just lie here in each other's arms until we are called for the reception dinner."

They savoured the moments in each other's arms before a knock on the door interrupted them. They descended the impressive staircase to be welcomed by a sea of smiles and loud clapping from the guests who were all in a jovial mood after copious glasses of wine and champagne. The sumptuous banquet began, with no expense spared in its preparation and presentation. Everyone, particularly to Great-Aunt Charlotte's delight, was having a wonderful time. The speeches, toasts, congratulations, and dancing passed in a mist of immense joy for William and Jane. Suddenly, people were leaving and saying their goodbyes. The entire day that had taken so many weeks of planning had passed in what seemed like moments to

William and Jane, yet the moments would be captured in both their heads for all eternity.

It was Great-Aunt Charlotte and Uncle Charles who were the last to leave, explaining that they would be away for five or six days at their house in Leigh Woods. They discussed the new promised bridge being built by Brunel, which would save so much time and be far safer in wintertime when the roads could be quite dangerous. Great-Aunt Charlotte kissed them both and wished them a safe journey to Ottery St Mary. William shook Uncle Charles by the hand and thanked him for such a generous wedding gift, and Jane kissed him on his whiskery cheek.

Jane and William were finally alone, and they appreciated the long ascension back up the staircase towards the bliss they had both yearned for. The servants had been warned not to disturb the couple under any circumstances.

It was William who was the first to awake the following day, simply staring at his beautiful bride before drawing the curtains, something which would normally be done by the housemaid, but this was a time for intimacy, thought William. The sun was shining, and the grand Georgian square had already been busy for several hours. William looked at his watch; it was half past eight, much later than he was used to rising on a morning. But then this was exceptional, and he looked at his new bride once more. He felt quite exhausted and relieved; the weight of both the impending wedding and what had happened in Ludlow was now hopefully behind him, and he felt like the happiest man alive.

William crossed the large, carpeted room and gently nudged Jane. "Jane darling, it's time to get up," said William. Jane stirred and opened her eyes. The sunlight streaming through the windows temporarily blinded her until William came into focus and gently kissed her on the lips. "It's half past eight," said William and smiled. "I think we should perhaps get up and go for breakfast." Jane looked panicked. "Whatever will people think?" she fretted. "Don't worry, darling, everyone will understand. It was our wedding night, remember?" winked William. Jane laughed, kissed him, and nuzzled into William's side.

William and Jane quickly got ready for the day, with William washing and shaving while Jane indulged in the luxury of running hot water. They then headed downstairs to be greeted by head butler Angus McGill, who welcomed them and asked if they would like breakfast.

William eagerly replied that they would, and Angus led them to the dining room, which had been transformed since the previous evening. While William and Jane enjoyed their breakfast, Angus and his staff had taken advantage of their mistress's absence and enjoyed a hearty meal themselves.

After breakfast, William asked Angus to prepare a picnic for them and arrange for a carriage to take them to Durdham Downs near Clifton. The couple set off in the open carriage, enjoying the sunshine and passing through areas of Hotwells and Whiteladies before reaching The Downs. The groom parked the carriage in a shaded spot, and William and Jane settled down for their picnic near to a group of trees.

Meanwhile, the groom watered the horses and checked the parcel of food that Cook had given him, which included a bottle of ginger beer. He looked forward to enjoying the rest of the easy day.

The first day of marriage proved perfect for William and Jane as they enjoyed the warmth of the day and watched people out walking, young children playing, and open top coaches circulating around the vast area of The Downs. Young and not so young ladies in their finery, with parasols to protect their delicate pale skin, completed the picturesque view.

When the breeze picked up, William and Jane decided to pack up the rugs, picnic basket, and stroll back to their carriage where the groom was waiting. He took the rugs and basket from William and promptly opened the carriage door for them. The groom directed the carriage back towards the top of Blackboy Hill where he could stop briefly to water the horses at the troughs that the "Ladies of the city" had kindly installed for their welfare. As coming up was very steep, there was also a highly decorated gentlemen's convenience, but nothing for the ladies. Going down was easier for both the horses and carriages as long as they had good brakes.

They soon returned to Queen's Square and retired to their room, requesting Rosemary be sent up to help with the packing for their journey to Devon the following day. The couple then went to the drawing room for afternoon tea. A delightful display of homemade cake, scones, preserve, and butter awaited them, which they enjoyed with great gusto. The fresh air of The Downs, away from the smells and filth of the city, had given them an unusually large appetite.

Mrs Duncan the housekeeper returned with the evening dinner menu, and William and Jane chose roast lamb and vegetables followed by a simple custard and jelly. "Mrs Duncan," said William, "could you please ask Mr McGill to come in? I'd like to go over tomorrow's arrangements with him. And could we please have breakfast for half-past seven?"

"Certainly, sir," said Mrs Duncan and hurried off to find Mr McGill. She had become quite taken with this young couple and wished them well, particularly after the terrible thing that had happened to the young man, which had made him so famous all over the country.

After speaking with Angus, William looked towards Jane knowingly, and they returned to their grand suite. After suppressing his desire for Jane for so long, William could not contain himself any longer and pulled Jane to him frantically, undoing the buttons at the back of her dress as he did so, but with little success: it was a skill he had yet to master.

"Careful," said Jane, stepping out of her dress, undoing the bodice beneath. William removed his jacket and quickly shed the rest of his clothes. Remarkably there was no shyness between them, such was the ease they naturally had in each other's company. They were both soon completely naked and William gently lifted her onto the bed, consummating their bodies within seconds, with complete abandonment, fulfilling a desire beyond their imaginations. Jane felt her body could take no more, and with her head slightly spinning with ecstasy, they both then fell into a deep slumber.

A sharp rap on the door from Rosemary awakened the couple, advising them that dinner would be served at half past six. She made no attempt to enter the room, as she guessed they might be preoccupied.

Dinner was excellent as usual, and they decided to have an early night as they would have a remarkably busy and tiring day tomorrow. Jane was looking forward to their honeymoon in Devon. Whilst William was a well-travelled businessman, Jane had never been far outside of Bristol in all her life and thought of it as a romantic adventure with the man she loved. With thoughts of the wedding and all that had happened over the last couple of days, her mind was wide awake, and she hardly slept a wink that night, with thoughts endlessly circling in her head.

Chapter 15

In what seemed like a blink of an eye to Jane, a knock on the door advised them that breakfast would soon be ready. They both reluctantly left their wonderfully comfortable bed and hurried to get ready, with Jane taking advantage of the plentiful supply of hot water and a bath while William carefully shaved and bathed after Jane in lavender-scented water. Their ablutions soon finished, they rushed downstairs, almost bumping into Rosemary who was waiting outside to pack their bags and belongings.

After a hearty breakfast, their luggage was called for, and a hamper prepared by Mrs Duncan was about to be loaded onto the waiting coach. All the servants were lined up, with Angus McGill and the housekeeper at the head of the queue.

"Have a safe journey, sir, madame," said Angus with a slight bow, followed by a domino of bows and curtsies by the rest of the servants.

"Thank you," said William, and he thanked everyone individually for their attention and for looking after him and his dear lady wife so well over the last few days. It was rare, thought Angus, for visitors to offer such politeness to the servants, as they were often taken for granted.

William and Jane boarded the barouche, and the clatter of hooves was heard on the cobbles of the square as the couple left for the post office and their onward journey to Exeter. It was a busy morning, with other coaches for various destinations waiting in line, people rushing everywhere, and porters offering to carry passengers' luggage for a small fee of coppers. William thought he spotted Isaac, the young coachman who had taken them to Redland and Clifton when he and Henry had returned from Ludlow. The memory of his last departure to the Midlands brought the past racing back, and his thoughts were suddenly elsewhere. Standing motionless with a blank expression, Jane nudged William back to the present. "My darling, what is it? You seemed like you were in a trance."

"It's nothing, my love, just the fatigue from the excitement of the wedding catching up with me, I think." Jane smiled and seemed reassured.

They soon found their coach, and the footman who had accompanied them brought over their luggage to be loaded. William thanked him, and he doffed his hat. The coach line agent checked their names, and they were soon on their way, passing through many villages and small towns. Jane, who had rarely left the city, found it all quite fascinating. The fields were full of cattle and sheep, and she even saw some huge oxen drawing a plough. "Look, William, at that huge beast! I have never seen such a large creature." Everyone in the coach leaned forward to the nearside window to catch a glimpse as they went by. "I have seen one working on the Cirencester Estate," said William, "when I visited Uncle Frederick there. It must have been at least two feet taller than its handler." Hayricks were being built, as countryfolk were preparing for winter, which was not too far away.

They had comfort stops on the way for food and exercise, if required, and the change-over of horses. It was a very bumpy ride in parts, so when the postilion blew his horn to signal an inn, most passengers were keen to take advantage of the hostelry's facilities.

There were only five passengers travelling inside the coach, including themselves; a married couple who were returning to Taunton, where they lived, and a portly middle-aged man who would accompany them all the way to Exeter. The husband introduced himself and his wife, who was easily twice his size, and William thanked their lucky stars that only five were travelling as she was taking up the space of two. His business was watch and clock-making and repairs and the couple had been visiting relatives in Bristol at the same time as conducting some business. They were a jolly pair and kept the conversation going for quite some time before the journey started to take its toll, and the two couples felt a bit drowsy. The other portly gentleman who had introduced himself as Fred Scrivens buried his head in a book throughout the journey. William could not see what the title was, but obviously, the gentleman was enthralled with the read.

There were an equal number of passengers on top, but all gentlemen dressed for the elements, plus two coachmen. Luckily the weather was very mild, and there was no sign of rain.

It was late afternoon by the time they arrived in Taunton, and there was a change of passengers, with the clockmaker and his ample wife alighting from the carriage. It was a cheery "Goodbye, and best wishes for a safe journey," and they were off.

The passengers on the journey took the opportunity to visit the inn and have some food and drink. William and Jane had enjoyed Mrs Duncan's hamper during the journey, and even offered to share the large slices of pork pie with their fellow passengers. However, after several hours, they decided to have a light meal of good Somerset cheese, bread, and a tankard of excellent homemade cider from the inn, which they thoroughly enjoyed.

As they continued their journey to Exeter, two new passengers, Mr David and Mr Abraham White, joined them. The brothers were both in the ironmongery business and looked almost identical, wearing the same colour and style of clothes and hats, which they removed upon seeing Jane. William thought they reminded him of characters from Charles Dickens' *Pickwick Papers* due to their rotund build and plump, rosy cheeks. The conversation flowed between the gentlemen all the way to Exeter, discussing their common interest in the ironmongery business. During several stops on the way, William shared his thoughts with Jane about the brothers' resemblance to the characters from the book.

Upon arriving in Exeter, they stayed the night at an inn before continuing their journey to Ottery St Mary the next day. After an excellent dinner and a good night's sleep, they found a coachman named Wilkins, who agreed to a return fare of half a guinea to their destination. They spent the last leg of their journey admiring the Devon countryside and the little villages and hamlets they passed through. When they reached the small town of Ottery St Mary, Wilkins stopped to ask a local resident for directions, and they soon afterwards arrived at their destination, an imposing but not huge residence on the edge of town named Willow Tree House. Jane wondered how it got its name.

No sooner had the coach stopped than the front door opened, and a rosy-cheeked, smiling face greeted them. "Welcome to Willow Tree House, my dears. We have been expecting you."

Chapter 16

"I am Liza Redfern, the housekeeper, and this is Sarah, the housemaid, sir, and we will be looking after you. Let me take your coats, and Sarah will look after your luggage."

Wilkins appeared to be struggling up the pathway with the luggage, but he was quite used to it and was stronger than he looked. "Where do you want the trunks, Missy?" asked Wilkins as Sarah appeared in the doorway.

"In the hallway will be fine," said Sarah. Wilkins obliged and was rewarded with a few coppers that Liza had given Sarah beforehand. "Will you be coming back in a couple of weeks for the Master?" said Sarah.

"I certainly will, and I hope to be here about 10 o'clock sharp, you can depend on it," said Wilkins, and then he was gone.

Back in the house, Liza showed William and Jane into the drawing room; a lovely, comfortable, sunny room overlooking the back gardens. "What a beautiful room," said Jane. William agreed as they settled into some very accommodating armchairs, that suited the whole peaceful ambience of the room.

"Now, sir, madame," said Liza. "Would you like some tea and cakes now, or would you prefer to go to your room to refresh yourselves after your journey?"

"I think we will have the tea first if you please, Liza," said William, "and we will go to our room afterward."

"Very well, sir," and Liza hurried off to the kitchen where Sarah was waiting.

"What do you think of them?" said Sarah.

"They are genuinely nice people, and he called me Liza, which I prefer to Mrs Redfern. Now let us get their tea. They must be parched."

The house was not as grand as Queen's Square, but it was still quite spacious and had large gardens attached. William and Jane were happy to be there at the kindness of Jane's cousins, Alexander and Grace who were on business in Lisbon. Jane was looking out of the window over a large expanse of lawn and flower borders, which swept to the right of her vision into what could be another secret garden. From the corner of her eye, Jane was suddenly aware of a figure on her left side busy doing something. It was just at that moment there was a knock on the door, and Liza entered with the tea and a selection of cake and sandwiches. William put the book he was looking at back on the shelf and thanked Liza.

"Liza," said Jane, "who is that in the garden?"

"That will be Jed," said Liza. "He deals with all the gardens with that lad of his and also helps with heavy lifting in the house now that Peter Hawkins, our old butler, retired. The master will be looking for a new butler and footman when they return from abroad. We do not have a coachman as the master prefers to drive himself, which is why there was no one to meet you in Exeter, madame." Liza curtseyed and left the room, leaving William and Jane to enjoy an excellent tea of homemade Devon produce.

William rang the servant's bell, and Liza soon appeared. "That was excellent," said Jane, and William agreed. "Would it be possible Liza, as we are both feeling quite tired from the journey, for us to retire to our room, if you are able to lead the way?" enquired William.

"Certainly, sir, and your luggage has already been taken to your room by Jed. I can send Sarah to help you unpack, madame, if you like?"

"That is quite alright," said Jane. "I am sure I can manage." That is a first, thought Liza to herself. Most guests never lifted a finger.

As they were guided to their room, they realised that the house was much bigger than it appeared from the front. It went back quite a long way with at least seven bedrooms, with additional servants' quarters on the upper floors. There were outbuildings and a large stable block that went from the house into a cobbled courtyard.

The room was beautifully furnished, with a number of paintings that had no doubt come back from Alexander's trips to Spain and Portugal. After closing the door behind them, William pulled Jane towards him in a frenzy of passion that had been building up over the last couple of days. As their lips met, Jane felt herself stir, and she could feel William pressing against her. William was undoing the buttons to her dress and, at the same time, tearing off his jacket and releasing the buttons on his trousers. The top half to Jane's dress and her bodice were already off and on the floor as William reached under her skirt to release the rest of Jane's clothing. He gently pushed her back onto the huge bed, and Jane let out a gasp.

As they melted together, there was an explosion of bodies that seemed to last forever. Minutes later, they gently pulled apart, lying side by side with hands entwined. "William," said Jane. "I love you so much."

"I love you too, Jane ... I must be the luckiest man in England." After making love for the second time, they both fell asleep in each other's arms. Their heavy doze was halted an hour or so later by the soft dinging of William's fob watch.

They both washed, changed, and went down to dinner. Afterwards, they retired to the drawing room to enjoy a smooth sherry that Alexander had shipped from his cellars in Jerez. "I am so pleased we were able to come on this honeymoon, William. Are you?" Jane asked.

"I certainly am," said William. He looked pensive, reflecting, "After what has been a terrible year, I am now in a lovely house and town, with my beautiful bride. What else could I ask for?"

"Tomorrow," said Jane. "I am going to ask Mrs Redfern all about the town. I am sure there must be some interesting places to see."

"An excellent idea, my love," said William. "And while you are doing that, I will take a stroll around the garden. I am sure there are many parts of it that remain unexplored."

"It's been such a long but exciting day," Jane concluded as she looked into his eyes and thought to herself that every moment had been wonderful.

Chapter 17

The next morning, Jane visited Mrs Redfern in the kitchen after breakfast to ask her some questions about the town. William left Jane to it and went out to the gardens to look for Jed, who he was sure had a great deal of knowledge about both the gardens and the town.

When Jane arrived in the kitchen, she found it to be quite large with everything a good cook would need, including an open fire with two large ovens for cooking and a warming oven. There was even a mechanical spit for large roasts should the occasion arise. Jane took a seat at the large kitchen table where all the servants had their meals, and Liza sat opposite her.

"Well," said Liza, "what would you like to know? I am a local girl, born and bred, and there's not much I don't know about what's going on."

"I would like to know about anything interesting about the town." requested Jane.

Liza began by telling Jane that there were about four thousand people living in the town and nearby, with quite a few working in the silk factory, farming, running shops, and trades, making cheese, and working in service, such as herself. She went on to explain that the town was once owned by the pixies, so legend has it, and that they left when the humans arrived. The humans built the church and installed the bells. The pixies believed that every time the bells rang, some of them would die, so they captured the bell ringers and held them hostage in a cave. But luckily, they escaped and continued to ring the church bell, so the pixies left, defeated, and the humans took over.

Jane burst out laughing. "You don't really believe that Liza. You are pulling my leg," said Jane.

"I certainly do, and it's bad luck to mock the pixies, I can tell you. Every midsummer, the children dress as pixies and have a party," said Liza.

"What else?" asked Jane, eager to hear all the tales.

"Well, there's the 'Fire Barrels', which all the young, strong men do on the 5th of November," replied Liza.

Before Jane could enquire further Liza added, "Shall we have a cup of tea, madame? All this talking is making me thirsty." Liza went to a large cabinet and retrieved an ornate, lockable mahogany box, which she opened using one of the many keys attached to her waist. Inside the box, there was a silver spoon attached to the inner lid. Liza then fetched a large china teapot and placed it next to a large kettle.

"I always warm the pot first, madame," said Liza. "It gives a better flavour to the tea."

"I will remember that" thought Jane to herself, as she had never made a cup of tea or anything else in her life. She had never needed to.

Meanwhile, Sarah was back in the kitchen, washing up all the breakfast crockery and making quite a noise about it.

"You be careful with that bone China, my girl. If you break anything, it will come out of your wages," scolded Mrs Redfern.

"Yes, Mrs Redfern," replied Sarah, who had now put some very pretty porcelain cups on the table from the huge collection in the dresser cabinet. She also brought out some fresh milk in a silver jug and a matching sugar bowl and spoons.

"As soon as you finish the washing up, Sarah, I expect you would like a cup of tea?" said Mrs Redfern.

"Thank you, Mrs Redfern," said Sarah appreciatively. Tea was a rare treat for her, and she had only been allowed to have it once since she joined the household.

"Now, back to the barrels," said Liza, redirecting the conversation. "It all started in the 17th century, and I believe it has to do with Guy Fawkes. Old wooden barrels are filled with tar and oil and set alight by young men who carry them down the High Street until they burn out. It's quite a sight to see, I can tell you.

Then there is the ghost of John Coke that wanders down the church aisle at night, so they say," continued Liza. "But I haven't seen him, and I don't want to either, thank you very much. He was a soldier, and his brother murdered him, but I do not know the circumstances that caused such a terrible thing. And of course, there is the famous astronomical clock, which is hundreds of years old, and the beautiful timber roof that dates to around 1260.

There is also the Chanters House," said Liza, pausing briefly. "It's the school that King Henry VIII started, but there's nothing left of the original building. Though King's School still exists. Oliver Cromwell also stayed there for a while, and the Coleridge family owns it now. Samuel Taylor Coleridge, the poet, was born there, but he died a few years ago in London and was buried there, though they do say his heart is buried in the churchyard somewhere. But I do not know if that is true, my dear. They also say that he was addicted to opium, and that is what killed him, but I do not know if that is true either. Well, I cannot think of anything else now, but if anything comes to mind, I will let you know," concluded Liza.

"Thank you very much, Liza, for sharing your knowledge of the area," said Jane, intrigued. "How long have you been in service here?"

"About seven years, madame," replied Liza. "The family has been very kind to me and my son. I am a widow now, as my husband was killed in a farm accident. So, it is just me and my son John, who is lucky to be in service with Colonel James Coleridge at Heath Court. He looks very smart in his uniform. I see him on his Sundays off, and we go to St Mary's Church and then come back here for tea, which madame allows."

"Thank you, Liza, for your time. William and I shall try to see as much as possible while we are here," said Jane. "You are always busy, and we appreciate your knowledge of the area."

"You're very welcome, my dear," replied Liza, feeling grateful for the appreciation. Jane smiled, thanked Mrs Redfern, and excused herself before leaving the kitchen to find William talking to Jed.

"Morning, madame," said Jed, taking off his cap and bowing slightly to reveal a white bald head with a distinctive white line separating it from his tanned weather-beaten face.

"I hope my husband has not been keeping you from your work, Jed," Jane teased.

My Lord thought Jed. Madame knows my name, and she is a pretty young thing as well.

"Jed has been giving me a tour of the grounds," said William. "It has a walled garden for vegetables and fruit, and a glass house with a large separate area for flowers and another with seats and rose beds. Most of it is hidden from the house because of the bend in the lawn, so it is very deceptive. There is also a small meadow that leads down to the river and the willow trees, which answers your question about the house, Jane. Jed was telling me they are particularly useful too, as they weave the branches to make windbreaks for the gardens, and they also make good bean sticks. I have decided to try and grow some vegetables and plant some fruit trees on the terraced garden in our new house, and Jed has given me some excellent tips." Jed's cheeks reddened.

"Now mind not to forget to use plenty of well-rotted horse compost," said Jed, "that be the secret." William and Jane thanked Jed and headed back to the house.

That afternoon, William and Jane took a casual stroll to St Mary's Church, and both agreed it looked like a beautiful cathedral on a smaller scale, a bit like Exeter Cathedral. As soon as they saw it, they felt it to be a special place, and as they entered the large oak doors, there was an instant feeling of peace. Jane remembered the story of the ghost, and they searched for the effigy of John Coke, which they soon found in its alcove, and Jane relayed the whole eerie story to William.

Over the remainder of their honeymoon, they took strolls along the river and met many of the friendly townsfolk and visited other little places that Mrs Redfern suggested they might like to see.

William thought Jane looked more beautiful than ever, quite radiant, in fact, apart from the last couple of mornings when she had not felt up to joining William on the walks and preferred to stay at home doing some embroidery she had brought from Bristol. William did not mind and took the opportunity to visit some of the local pubs, in particular, The Volunteer and The King's Arms, both of which served excellent local ciders for which he had developed a taste.

There was a hush and conversation stopped for a few seconds when he went into The Volunteer Arms for the first time. He was a stranger in town, but word had soon got round that there were visitors at Willow Tree House. William's appearance inevitably attracted some brief stares, but a mixture of politeness and embarrassment caused them to soon look away. However, Devon folk being direct asked the question as to how William had got his scar. It was the landlord serving William who broached the subject: "May I ask sir, how you got that injury? Serving the Queen?"

William had gotten used to the question, but it rarely happened in Bristol now as everyone was aware of what had happened to him through the newspapers and general conversation. William retold his story as succinctly as possible while the whole pub fell silent. "My God, sir," exclaimed the landlord, "it makes you wonder if anyone can ever be safe in their own bed. I hope the villain gets his due punishment, whatever it may be! And the cider is on me, sir."

The buzz of conversation continued as quickly as it had stopped, and the question was never asked again. Thereafter, William was made to feel very welcome on his subsequent visits. Within 24 hours, everyone in the small town knew anyway, and those with access to the Exeter newspapers suddenly remembered the horrific story from a few months ago.

As William returned to Willow Tree House, he was welcomed by Mrs Redfern. "Madame is resting, sir, and has requested that dinner be served at seven o'clock this evening, if that's agreeable to you, sir?" she said.

"Certainly," replied William. "But may I trouble you for some tea in the drawing room, please Liza?"

"Right away, sir," said Mrs Redfern.

Sarah was chopping up some mint to accompany the lamb they were serving that evening. "Leave that for a minute, Sarah," ordered Mrs Redfern. "And get me some China out of the dresser. The gentleman would like a cup of tea. Get the Meissen set with the little mauve flowers on it, but only one cup, and be careful. That costs more than my year's wages," she exclaimed. Mrs Redfern gave Sarah the key and checked that the kettle was near boiling.

"I can't find them," said Sarah frantically.

"They're on the right-hand side of the main service," said Mrs Redfern, quite exasperated. "You should know by now. Everything has a place, and everything in its place, as my mother used to say. Remember that my girl. I do not know what goes on inside your head at times. Be careful and hand the teapot over."

"Sorry, Mrs Redfern," said a forlorn-faced Sarah, nearly in tears.

Mrs Redfern gently warmed the pot, unlocked the tea caddy, and put in two spoonsful before adding the water. "One per person and one for the pot," was her recipe for a good cup of tea. "Let that stand to brew for a minute," she said as she relocked the caddy and gave it to Sarah to put back in the dresser. She then carefully arranged the teapot, the cup, milk jug, sugar tongs, and sugar on the serving tray. "I will take this in, and we will have something ourselves."

Sarah was just finishing the mint sauce, and Mrs Redfern took a sip before Sarah put it in the pantry. "That's very good, my girl. You are beginning to learn at last," she said. Sarah felt a slight blush on her cheeks as she normally received little praise from Mrs Redfern.

William finished his tea and cake and went upstairs to see how Jane was feeling. She was up and dressed and looked as lovely as ever. "How are you feeling now, darling?" he asked, as he pulled Jane into his arms.

"I feel fine," said Jane. "And I am looking forward to dinner this evening. I have put some of our belongings into our trunk and bags, ready for our return home. I cannot believe we only have one more day left. Oh William, I have had such a glorious time here over the last two weeks. It was so kind of Alexander and Grace to let us stay in their lovely house. I will remember it always."

"I have had a wonderful time too, my darling," said William, kissing Jane gently on the lips and forehead and holding her tight. "Where have you been this afternoon?" asked Jane, and William explained his visits to the pub and conversations with the locals.

William washed and changed his shirt before going down to dinner, and Jane thought how handsome he looked. Even though still faintly visible, Jane hardly noticed the scar that had stretched from ear to ear as it had faded to a light pink, from the deep red of the original wound.

William and Jane enjoyed a splendid dinner consisting of fresh vegetable soup from the garden, followed by seasoned lamb, buttered potatoes, and more vegetables. For dessert, they ate a mouth-watering apple pie and fresh cream. Jane expressed her desire to find a cook as good as Mrs Redfern when they returned home to Bristol, to which William agreed, mentioning that they needed to prioritise their servant situation upon their return.

William rang the table bell, and Mrs Redfern promptly entered the room. William complimented her cooking and repeated his wife's desire to find someone so accomplished for themselves. Liza's cheeks glowed, followed by a quick curtsey as she left the room.

The following morning, with most of their packing done, William and Jane took a stroll around the town and visited St Mary's Church before returning to Willow Tree House for a light lunch. Afterwards, Jane decided to rest, while William went back to the sitting room to read his book. Mrs Redfern appeared and asked if he required anything else. William requested a small tankard of the cider they had the other evening and asked if they could prepare a hamper of food for their journey the following day. Mrs Redfern nodded with, "Of course, sir."

As William prepared to leave, he approached Liza and declared his immense gratitude for her exceptional service during their honeymoon. "Please accept this as a token of our appreciation." as he pressed a full gold sovereign into her hand.

Liza opened her palm and gazed at the shiny large coin. She had never owned such a thing in her entire lifetime. She just stared. "Lord," exclaimed Liza. "I cannot accept it, sir. It is my job, and the master would be annoyed if he found out! I'm sure I'd get into trouble."

"Then it will be just our little secret, Liza. I do not want to hear anything more about it," said William. Liza curtsied and left the room in a daze, still looking at the sovereign in the palm of her hand as if it were all a dream. It had to be a secret, and she would tell no one.

William took another sip of cider and thought about tomorrow. He hoped that Wilkins, the coachman, would arrive on time as they did not want to miss their connection from Exeter to Bristol. They had dinner that evening and retired early for their busy journey tomorrow. The country air certainly suited them, and William felt he had not slept so well for quite some time. Back in Bristol, with more noise and his frequent nightmares, he would wake up in a sweat, often screaming out, with Jane having to comfort him back to sleep. In contrast, during their honeymoon, William had begun to feel safer, more reassured, and unconsciously, this was helping him to sleep more soundly, with only one night when he had experienced a bad dream. He thought that the sanctuary of Ottery St Mary would help him adjust back to the life he enjoyed before the trip to Ludlow when he was carefree, ambitious, and in love.

Chapter 18

They rose early the next day and finished packing before going down to breakfast. Liza had called Jed in from the garden, who had brought down the heavy trunk and baggage. Jed was sorry to hear they were leaving so soon. It did not seem five minutes since the couple arrived, and he had enjoyed his conversations with the gentleman.

Wilkins the coachman was as good as his word and arrived on time. Mrs Redfern, Sarah, Jed, and his son were all lined up to see them off. William shook their hands and thanked them. As the newlyweds left everyone waved frantically and wished them well. "I hope they will be very happy in their new life," said Mrs Redfern, with emotion. "They deserve it if anyone does."

As the carriage pulled out of sight Mrs Redfern remarked, "Right, well let's get on with it. Doing nothing will not buy the baby a new bonnet, as they say! My girl, we are going to do some shopping tomorrow. I have a surprise for you." Liza was going to buy Sarah a new straw bonnet she had seen, with little violet flowers all around the rim. The poor soul did not have much, and she was going to share her good luck of the new shiny sovereign William had given her.

After William and Jane had left, she spent some time sat in her kitchen just looking at starting at the golden coin. She had never held so much money in her hand at any one time. She had seen her Great-Uncle Zebedee with sovereigns in his hand after selling some of his cattle, but it did not last long after paying off debts and buying new calves to bring on, and hopefully make a profit.

Luckily, it was a bright and dry day with only a slight chill in the air as William and Jane made their way back to Exeter. They were making good time and Jane commented that the journey seemed to be quicker than the outward one. Upon arriving at their destination, they disembarked where they were due to pick up the coach to Bristol, and William paid Wilkins for his service.

The innkeeper had noticed their arrival and enquired if they were going on to Bristol. William confirmed their destination and produced his documents. "That's all in order, sir. Thank you," said the innkeeper. "I will arrange for your luggage to be brought in for safekeeping until the coach arrives. Exeter is quite a safe place, but we do have our share of vagabonds."

William and Jane were then led into the smoky pub and shown to a private area where it was acceptable for ladies travelling to sit. William ordered some ciders, and the waiter soon returned, asking if they would be taking dinner. "We have some roast pork turning on the spit, with potatoes, carrots, greens, and apple sauce, sir," said the waiter. Turning to Jane, William asked what she thought, and she suggested they have a meal now and save the rest of the hamper Mrs Redfern had provided for later. William agreed and ordered two small portions. The pork was cooked to perfection, and they left little on their plates.

Soon the post horn sounded, and they were on their way again. Within an hour or so, they entered Somerset and noticed the slightly different architecture of the buildings along the way with less cob, thatch and limewash displaced with more stone and brick dwellings. After a few hours and a rest stop, William and Jane opened the hamper, which was full of flagons of cider, pork pies, fresh cheese, bread, ham, and the famous fruitcake that Mrs Redfern had promised. After indulging in all the delicious cuisine over the last week or so, William felt his waistcoat had become a bit tight and mentioned it to Jane, who smiled and said she thought her bodice might need to be let out.

As they continued their journey, Jane could not help but wonder why return journeys always seemed shorter. She had never travelled this far before, and the trip home gave her a chance to reflect on what a marvellous adventure it had been, one she would surely never forget. She felt content and happy as she glanced up at William, feeling proud of her new husband.

When they reached Taunton, a new passenger joined them inside the coach. He doffed his hat to Jane and William and introduced himself as Mr Michael Haines. He was well-dressed in a country style designed to last and give good service. Mr Haines was travelling to Bristol to see his sister in Bedminster, who had recently recovered from cholera, by the grace of God, he insisted. Miraculously, no one else in the family had been afflicted by the terrible disease, which was prone to affect the citizens of Bristol from time to time and take away many poor souls. It spares no one he lamented, neither rich nor poor.

It was soon discovered that Mr Haines was a carpenter and joiner who employed several people in Taunton, including two apprentices. Like William, he was tall and slim in build. As the owner of the business, he could afford to take time off to visit his only sister but had left his wife and children at home, thinking it wise to keep them out of the city. William agreed, and that was the last they spoke as Mr Haines promptly fell asleep until their arrival in Bridgwater. Only the sound of the post horn startled him; otherwise, he would have slept all the way to Bristol as his snoring was deep and loud. Jane found it amusing as he suddenly stopped and started again with a little jolt, like one of the little piglets she saw with its mother and siblings in a field in Ottery St Mary.

After Bridgwater, Jane began to feel tired herself and rested her head against William's shoulder, soon joining Mr Haines in slumber. William looked down at her, wondering whether Jane was going down with something and whether she should see the family doctor when they got home. It was not only the sickness that occurred several times when they were on holiday, but she also seemed to have felt fatigued quite quickly in the last few days, which was not like Jane at all. Her energetic countenance had been one of the qualities that had first attracted him to her.

As they finally reached the outskirts of Bristol, William noticed how much busier it seemed compared to Devon, with people going about their business everywhere in a rush, unlike the solitude and tranquillity of Ottery St Mary. Momentarily, William felt a small unease in the pit of his stomach as some of his old anxiety returned. The carriage rattled down the cobbled streets of Bedminster and then the last half mile to their destination. The post horn sounded, and they soon came to a stop outside the busy post office.

William's spirits instantly lifted again, and his nervousness subsided as he saw a familiar face. His brother Henry was waiting for them. "Welcome home, dear brother. Dear sister," giving William a hug and kissing Jane on the cheek. "We have all so missed you! It seems ages since the wedding. I trust you had a wonderful time?"

"Yes, we certainly have," said William, squeezing Jane's waist. "It could not have been better."

"Well, things have been moving on here, and I have some good news and some not so good news but let's get to the cab first, and I can explain on the way. I spotted Isaac in the rank, so I have hired him to take us to Redland."

William queried, "What? About our new house in Kingsdown?" with a puzzled and concerned look.

"Do not worry, dear boy. I will explain everything," said Henry with his usual cheery smile. Isaac had arrived, smart as usual, lowered his cap, and started to load their luggage. He recognised them all and hoped he might catch a glimpse of his sweetheart, Cassie, the maid. He lit the lamps on the coach, and they were soon on their way.

Chapter 19

"Right," said William impatiently. "Tell me, Henry. What exactly has happened?"

"Well, unfortunately," said Henry, "there has been a slight disagreement within the late owner's family as to who should share in the sale proceeds. However, I have been assured by the lawyers that it will be sorted out satisfactorily within the next month."

"A month!" cried William. "But where will we live?" His apprehension rose once more.

"I am sorry to be the bearer of unwelcome news to you both. You are, of course, disappointed, but the good news is that all is not lost. I have been able to obtain a short lease on a nice furnished property in Portland Square, and you can move in tomorrow. It is actually owned by a cousin of Christopher George, who is away for the next six months at least and is delighted to have someone there to keep the home fires burning," explained Henry.

"I have also taken the liberty of arranging some servant interviews on Tuesday, which I am sure Jane can do with the help of Mrs Brooks. Oh, and the furniture and household requirements you bought for the Kingsdown house are all on hold awaiting your orders."

"Oh Henry, what ever would we do without you?" cried Jane. Both William and Jane now felt better about the original news that greeted them, and both palpably relaxed as their minds returned to thoughts of being reunited with their family. It did not take long to reach Redland, where they were greeted by Jane's father, brother Joseph, sister Mary, and Mrs Brooks. "It's so delightful to have you both safely home," chirped Mrs Brooks, "even if it is just a few days."

"Come in, come in," said John. "It's getting chilly out there." They handed their coats to Mrs Brooks, who was drying her tears. Jane leaned forward and gently kissed Grace Brooks on the cheek. They all moved into the drawing room, and as they did so, Cassie rushed to the front door where Isaac was heaving the luggage up the steps. They had been walking out for a month now and were besotted with each other. Isaac glanced up at the smiling Cassie.

"All right, me luvver?" asked Isaac.

"Better for seeing you me 'ansome," replied Cassie as Isaac transferred the final suitcase into the hallway.

He looked quickly around before stealing a little kiss, which immediately caused Cassie's cheeks to go red. "Will I see you again on Sunday?" asked Isaac, already knowing the answer.

"If you still want me to?"

"Course I do," said Isaac. "That goes without saying, and Da has said we can use the trap to go over Ashton way if we want to, and the weather's dry."

"That would be lovely," said Cassie as they heard footsteps coming out of the drawing room and quickly drew apart.

"I have your fare, young man, so you can be on your way. And Cassie, back to the kitchen please, young lady. We have tea to make, then prepare the dinner," said Mrs Brooks, who knew what was going on as Cassie, who could never keep a secret, had confided in her about her young man weeks ago. She had warned the young Cassie, whom she had now grown fond of, not to bring any shame upon the household with any silliness.

In the drawing room, everyone was asking question after question about the honeymoon. As an aside, Henry reminded William that he had received a number of letters which he had taken the liberty of bringing with him from home, as a couple looked quite important. He had left them on the desk in John's study.

"Then, please excuse me," said William. "I had better give them my attention," as he rose from his chair.

Mrs Brooks arrived with some tea and cake, announcing that dinner would be in about an hour.

"Thank you," said Jane. "And by the way, Grace, there is a hamper with our luggage which still has some good Devon food in it. Do you think you could look and use whatever you think fit?"

"Certainly, my dear," said Mrs Brooks, and went about her chores.

"William, dear, do have some tea and cake and look at your letters afterwards," said Jane.

William did as he was told, while all the gossip continued around him. He was distracted, though, by his own thoughts. He had urgent matters to attend to and must get back to business first thing on Monday morning. He told himself that he had been away far too long, but he did not hold a single regret. It had been a glorious time, and as he looked across to Jane, who was in deep conversation with her sister, he felt so lucky and blessed. Jane looked radiant, but he reminded himself again that he must contact the family doctor as a matter of urgency to come and examine her, although she had insisted, she felt so much better now.

Chapter 20

When William reached the study, he found a pile of correspondence waiting for him. He sorted through the letters, selecting the most important looking one and broke its official seal. It was from the clerk of the Shrewsbury assizes, advising him that a trial date had been set for the 23rd of March 1841, and that his presence would be required. William made a note of the date in his journal and took the letter with him into the drawing room.

As he entered the room, some of his old anxiety returned, but he composed himself quickly. "You were quite right, Henry. A date has been set for the trial next year, and I have to attend, of course," he said.

"It's been expected, but it will bring the terrible event back to us all, particularly you, William. But it has to be done, and that will be the end of it. I will go with you, of course," replied Henry.

The Mackreth siblings were always close, but the last year had only strengthened the bond between them.

"I need to write some letters to confirm my attendance, and one or two other things that need attention," said William. "Do you have any writing paper to spare, Mr Bright?"

"Yes, of course. There is some in the bottom left-hand drawer, with wax and envelopes if needed. And please do call me John!"

"Thank you, John," said William as he returned to the study.

William's first order of business was to write two letters – one to the clerk of the court confirming his attendance at the trial, and the other to his family doctor, Dr Jameson Barber, urgently requesting an examination of Jane. Once he finished the letters, the dinner gong rang, and William realised how hungry he was after such a long day. Before heading to the dining room, he stopped by the kitchen to ask Mrs Brooks to take care of posting one of the letters and hand-delivering the other to Dr Barber in Coldharbour Lane, which she assured him she would do first thing in the morning.

After a satisfying dinner, William and Jane retired to bed, sharing a lingering kiss before falling into a deep and restful sleep.

In the kitchen, Mrs Brooks and Cassie were busy putting away the crockery and setting up the dining table for breakfast when Mrs Brooks wondered why William might need a doctor. After making sure all the doors were locked, they both went to bed. Mrs Brooks changed into her nightgown and socks, blew out the candle. Just before drifting off, the thought occurred to her that Jane might be expecting. She could not help but smile before falling sound asleep.

On a Sunday morning, no one woke up particularly early, except for Mrs Brooks, who spent her extra time in bed thinking about the day's chores. The family planned to go to church in the morning, followed by a light lunch of sandwiches and refreshments, and then a full dinner in the evening. Cassie, on the other hand, continued to sleep until Mrs Brooks came into her room and shook her awake. Mrs Brooks gave her a message to deliver to Dr Barber in Coldharbour Lane and instructed her to return in time to change for church. When Cassie asked who was ill, Mrs Brooks told her it was none of her business and to get up, wash, and prepare breakfast.

After breakfast, Cassie took the letter to Dr Barber's residence and handed it to a snooty-looking maid who then disappeared to check for a reply from the master. Cassie impatiently waited, not wanting to be late for church. The maid returned with a written message from Dr Barber confirming that he would attend to Mrs Mackreth after 10 o'clock on Monday morning.

Cassie ran most of the way back home and delivered the message to Mrs Brooks, who then took it to William, now in the drawing room with Mr Bright. "Thank you, Grace," he said as he read the message and excused himself from John to see Jane, who was still dressing for church.

"The doctor will be here to see you just after 10 in the morning, Jane, and I am sure he will require Mrs Brooks to be with you," William said to Jane.

"Oh, William darling, is it necessary? I feel fine and not at all unwell," replied Jane.

"I will be much happier if you do," said William. "Just for my peace of mind."

"Very well," said Jane, who knew William had been worried about her since her bouts of sickness in Ottery St Mary. He seemed to fret over so many things lately.

William had to admit to himself that Jane did look a picture of health. The following day, William left early for work, being careful not to disturb his wife. At Christopher George and Co, he was greeted by Arthur Jenkins, the Chief Clerk who always made a point of being at work before anyone else.

"Good morning, sir. It is such a pleasure to have you back with us and looking so well," Arthur said.

"Thank you, Arthur," replied William. "Perhaps you would be so kind as to bring me up to date with how business is going?"

"Certainly, sir. It is going very well, if I may say so," said Arthur as he produced the ledgers for William to peruse. "Mr George told me that he might be a little late this morning as he had some other business to deal with in Corn Street but would see you as soon as he came in."

"Thank you, Arthur. I will ring for you as soon as I have finished going through the ledgers and taken a walk round the foundry," said William.

Arthur Jenkins was correct. The ledgers showed that business and profits were excellent. The whole foundry was a hive of activity, and William returned to the office just as Christopher arrived in a cab, as his own coach was being repaired. Christopher rushed towards William, giving his business colleague and friend a long embrace.

"William, dear chap, let us toast your return with a brandy!" exclaimed Christopher.

They both entered the office, where a fire was blazing away. Christopher went to his private cabinet and brought out the brandy with a couple of glasses, pouring out two generous measures.

"To you and your dear lady wife, a toast of good health and a happy life together," said Christopher as they clinked their glasses.

"The same to you and Elizabeth," responded William.

"Now, how was your honeymoon?" asked Christopher.

"Perfect," beamed William. "And before I forget, I must thank you for the temporary accommodation in Portland Square. I am sure we will be very comfortable there until the Montague Hill house is ready."

"Not at all, dear boy."

"Thank you, Christopher," replied William as he sipped his brandy. "I am grateful for your understanding and support. We are moving in tomorrow and Mrs Brooks will help Jane on a daily basis, hopefully to interview some servants on Wednesday. My brother Henry has made all the arrangements."

"Oh yes, young Henry! A splendid fellow," replied Christopher, as he remembered their trip to Ludlow.

"Indeed, I am very fortunate to have such a brother." William agreed and then hesitated. "There is something I must tell you." He looked grave. "I have received a summons to the assize courts in Shrewsbury on the 23rd of March next year."

"I see. Of course, you must go. Will you go alone?" enquired Christopher taking another sip of brandy.

"No. Henry will accompany me and possibly my other brother George."

"Excellent. You need as much support as you can get and the sooner this sorry matter is put to rest the better. Let me top up your brandy glass."

Chapter 21

Back at the Bright household, Dr Barber arrived punctually and was immediately taken up to Jane's bedroom. She was sitting in a chair adjacent to the bed, wearing a loose-fitting day dress, feeling a little nervous. However, Dr Barber was a kindly man with a soft-spoken voice so would soon put her at ease. He turned to Mrs Brooks and said, "You will stay, of course, while I examine your Mistress?"

"Oh, yes, sir, of course," replied Mrs Brooks, standing by the door.

Dr Barber had been the family doctor for many years and knew Jane from childhood. "Right, Jane, if you would lie on the bed and bring the top half of your dress down to your waist so I may examine you," he said.

Jane did as she was told and felt herself flush with embarrassment. Dr Barber asked her what symptoms she had to make her husband concerned about her health, and she explained that apart from some sickness when they were in Ottery St Mary, she now felt fine.

"What was the date of your marriage?" asked Dr Barber, making a note of the date on a notepad he had taken from his case. He placed his hand on her forehead and took out his stethoscope to listen to her chest.

"No temperature, and your heart and lungs sound perfectly normal. However, there is a slight swelling of the tummy. How often do you have to pass water?" Jane explained that she had needed to pass water a little more often than usual but had not given it any thought.

"Well, young lady, I think you are to become a mother. Congratulations! From the information you have given me and the symptoms you have, I would expect you to give birth about the end of May next year. There is one more test I can do to be doubly sure, and I will require a water sample first thing in the morning. I can get back to you in a couple of days with the results."

Jane hastily dressed with Mrs Brooks' help, not knowing what to say, while Mrs Brooks grinned broadly as her intuition had proved correct. "Oh Grace, I can't quite believe this has happened so quickly. Is it possible?" Jane looked slightly concerned. "I do hope William will be pleased. He has been through so much in the last year. I do hope he will be as happy as I am."

As Jane bid farewell to Dr Barber, she explained that from tomorrow, their new address would be Portland Square and wrote down the address for him.

"Thank you, Jane. You can now give the good news to your husband. Congratulations once again."

Jane was elated but also shaking inside with excitement. She ordered Mrs Brooks not to tell a soul until William returned that evening, and Mrs Brooks crossed her heart and said, "I hope to die." Her father John was in the study and did not ask why Dr Barber had called, but he had guessed from the commotion and knew he would be told in time. This would be his first grandchild.

William arrived home in a cab at half past six that evening, anxious to hear what the doctor had to say. Cassie answered the door, all smiles and, at the same time, trying to look behind William to see if it was Isaac who had driven him home. It was, and she managed a quick wave before closing the door and taking William's hat and coat.

William strode into the drawing room where Jane was waiting for him, while her father had made a diplomatic retreat to his study. William greeted Jane with a kiss. "So, tell me, what did Dr Barber say?"

Jane took a step back, looked into William's eyes, and said, "He believes I'm expecting," waiting for William's response.

William was speechless for a few seconds, realising he was going to be a father. "William, the doctor will confirm it in a few days, but he seemed quite certain," Jane said.

"Oh, Jane, thank you my darling. You have made me happier than I could ever imagine. Is everything going well, are you experiencing any problems?" William asked with a slightly worried look.

"I am perfectly fine," Jane said. "It's still early days, but the doctor explained that the nausea I'm feeling is due to the pregnancy."

"Are you happy, my love?" William asked.

"My darling William, I could not be happier," Jane replied. She pulled William close and kissed him passionately.

"I love you so much," William said. "We must tell the family immediately."

"Mrs Brooks already knows," Jane said, "but she has been sworn to secrecy. Let's tell father first."

Chapter 22

Despite having had a few too many sherries the night before to celebrate the news, everyone was up early the following day, as there was plenty to do. It was the first day of William and Jane's independent lives in their own home, and they were excited at the prospect.

Mrs Brooks had told Cassie of Jane's good news and that she would oversee the house whilst she was in Portland Square with the new Mrs Mackreth. It had been a difficult job to say it, and it would take some time for Mrs Brooks to get used to calling Jane the new Mrs Mackreth, as to her, Jane had always been Miss Jane.

"I have left the lamb and vegetable soup for the master's lunch on the side of the range, and I expect he will require it about 1 o'clock as usual. So, make sure the dining table is laid in time and serve it with the fresh bread that is in the pantry, and have some yourself, of course."

"Yes, Mrs Brooks," Cassie replied, feeling proud that she had been given the responsibility.

"I will be back late afternoon, hopefully to prepare dinner for this evening."

"Yes, Mrs Brooks," Cassie repeated.

William would be going to work as usual and knew that Henry would be at Portland Square mid-morning. Henry had arranged for an Isabella Dando and a Pamela Berry to arrive at 11 o'clock to be interviewed for the positions of cook/housekeeper and general housemaid, and Mrs Brooks would assist Jane with their suitability. Henry had done his homework, and both candidates came with good references. Coal, kindling, and lamp oil had been delivered to get the fires and oven going, and victuallers would be delivering supplies at mid-day. It was all good practice, Henry thought, for when they moved again to their permanent residence in Kingsdown.

Jane was sad to leave the home she had known all her life, but she was now the mistress of her own household. As the carriage made its way down the hill to the city and Portland Square, Jane turned to Mrs Brooks.

"I do not know how I would manage without you, Grace. I am so grateful that you are with me today."

"I am sure you will manage, Miss Jane. It is just strange and something new to get used to. That is life. A continual run of new circumstances that we must adapt to as we go," philosophised Mrs Brooks. "You know, though, I am not a million miles away if you need any help. My job today is to set everything up and make sure these women are suitable for your service."

"Thank you, Grace, thank you," Jane replied, her voice filled with gratitude. Mrs Brooks had noticed how Jane had begun to call her Grace, rather than the more formal Mrs Brooks, and it gave her a deep sense of belonging within the family.

The house in Portland Square was three stories tall, plus the servants' quarters in the attic. Everything was furnished quite expensively, thought Jane, and very homely.

"My first job will be to light the drawing room fire and get the stove going. Leave it to me," said Mrs Brooks.

Meanwhile, Henry showed Jane around the downstairs rooms. After lighting the fires, Mrs Brooks found a large linen cupboard and started to select bedding for the master bedroom and the servants' quarters, which she hoped would be occupied soon. The rooms were large, and even the servants' quarters had their own wardrobes, washstands, and rugs on the polished wooden floors.

Things have certainly come a long way from her early days in service, thought Mrs Brooks. "Whoever gets these positions will be very lucky," she exclaimed to herself. There were candleholders and a supply of tallow candles and lucifer matches in the washstand drawers. The kitchen was fully stocked, and there was everything a good cook and housekeeper would need. Mrs Brooks finished her checklist and went back downstairs to be met by Henry, who told her the two girls had arrived and were in the drawing room with Jane.

The two women were standing when Mrs Brooks entered the room and Jane introduced her as their senior housekeeper who would be assisting with the interview. Mrs Brooks had never been called that before and felt six feet tall. The one called Pamela Berry was 17 years of age and came from Radstock, south-east of the city, where she had been in service since she was 14, doing all the basic household duties for two elderly sisters. Due to a change in circumstances, she was now unemployed and desperately needed a position with accommodation. She had good references. Mrs Brooks asked her several questions and seemed happy with the answers.

Isabella Dando was an older woman of 28 who was a cook and housekeeper, learning her skills over several years from her elders until she achieved her position with landed gentry, a family in Luckington, Gloucestershire. Isabella had decided that country life was no longer for her, as she only saw her family once a year as they lived in Easton in Bristol and had a small market garden business. She had never married so was still a Miss. She also had a reference, and her previous employers were reluctant to see her leave their service. She was obviously skilled by the way she answered to Mrs Brooks' questions, and that was all that mattered.

Jane asked Miss Dando to step into the hallway for a moment while she and Mrs Brooks discussed the situation. Both Isabella and Pamela whispered together in the hallway so as not to be overheard and immediately thought they could be friends. They both shared the same opinion that they would like to work for the mistress in this household although they had not met the master yet, only Henry.

Jane and Mrs Brooks were in deep conversation, the references were good, and Mrs Brooks had asked all the questions she could think of. Jane was relying totally on her judgment. "I think they are both suitable," declared Mrs Brooks and promptly called the women back into the drawing room.

"We have explained your wages and conditions of the contract and would now like to offer you both a position," said Jane. "We are only at this address temporarily. My husband and I will be moving to our house in Kingsdown in due course, if it is agreeable for you to come with us. If not, please say so now!"

"Yes, please, madame," they both said in unison.

"Excellent," as Jane brought her hands together in a gentle clap. "My brother-in-law will order a cab to take you to your respective lodgings to collect your belongings."

Everything was falling into place so well, thought Jane, thanks to Henry and Mrs Brooks.

Before they left Mrs Brooks gave them a tour of the rainwater storage tank in the cellar and the pump that would bring the water up to the scullery, located next to the well. The stored water was much softer than the well water used for washing, while the latter would be used to top up the small tanks above the toilet closets. There was one downstairs for the servants and one off the first-floor landing upstairs. Montague House was due for additional improvements as soon as the legal matters were sorted out, including modern water closets. However, William had said that a new cesspit would be needed, as all foul water from the house went directly into the nearby River Frome.

Henry later came into the drawing room and asked if everything was in order as he had to go back to business. He promised to inform the rest of the family of the good news when he returned home that evening and reminded Jane how excited he was at the prospect of becoming an uncle. Jane hugged her brother-in-law and thanked him again for all he had done. Before leaving, he informed Jane that he had ordered a cab to take Mrs Brooks back home to Redland at 4 o'clock.

With just an hour left, Mrs Brooks went through with Jane the routine of running a household. She assured her that everything would be fine, as they were two experienced servants, and the house should run itself. She encouraged Jane not to be afraid to speak up if there was anything she was not happy with, as she was the mistress and in charge. Jane also reminded her that she was only a short carriage ride away and could call to see them anytime. When Mrs Brooks left, Jane gave her a kiss on both cheeks, and as she waved goodbye, she felt a tear run down her cheek. She swiftly rubbed it away and hurried back into the house, determined not to let William down.

A few days later, both women were back at Portland Square, Miss Dando with a bit more luggage than Miss Berry. They were shown to their rooms and told to be back in the kitchen as soon as possible, dressed in their new servants' attire. Their first job would be to get the kettles boiling and prepare a light lunch from the provisions that had been delivered.

Their luggage had already been taken up to their bedroom, and Jane busied herself unpacking all their personal belongings and putting them in the dresser drawers and the two large wardrobes. She was having a quiet cup of tea in the drawing room when Isabella knocked on the door and inquired about the time she should serve dinner. Jane informed her that her husband should be home by half-past six, so 7 o'clock should be quite in order. Isabella curtseyed and left.

Jane could not help but notice how tall and pretty Isabella was, with her brown hair kept in a bun, fair complexion, blue-green eyes, and a nice smile. She wondered why Isabella had never married, but as long as she performed her duties, it was none of her business, and she thought it would be rude to ask. In comparison, Pamela was much shorter, with almost black hair and chestnut brown eyes, and a cheeky look that reminded her of Cassie in Redland. Jane felt sure she would get on well with both of them

William arrived home on time, and Pamela answered the door with a polite "Good evening, sir," taking William's hat, coat, and gloves. "Mistress is in the drawing room, sir."

"Thank you," said William and hurried into the room. Jane stood up to greet William, and he immediately pulled her to him, kissing her ardently as Jane responded. "Oh, how I've missed you," said William.

"I am sure Henry had told me, "Said William, "but I had forgotten! Please remind me again. Isabella Dando is the older one and is the cook/housekeeper, and the shorter, younger one who answered the door is Pamela Berry, the general housemaid?"

"Yes, exactly. Isabella has already cooked this evening's dinner, and it smells delicious," said Jane. They went into the kitchen, and Jane formally introduced William to Isabella and Pamela. William remarked that everything seemed to have gone very smoothly thanks to everyone's help and that they had been exceptionally lucky with the servants. "I think, Jane," said William, pausing and reaching across for her hand, "under the circumstances, we will also take on a housemaid whose duties will be to look after you. We can afford it, and we have enough servants' quarters here and at Montague."

"If you think so, William, although today has proven that we can manage very well."

"Yes, I agree, but things are changing, and Pamela would not be able to give all her time to you as she has other responsibilities under Isabella."

"Very well, my darling."

Chapter 23

The Mackreth household were all naturally delighted at the news of Jane's pregnancy, and Great-Aunt Charlotte saw it as the perfect excuse to throw a party for the couple.

Meanwhile, in the Bright household, Cassie's thoughts were consumed with her upcoming afternoon off and meeting with Isaac. It was just her, the master, young Mary and Mrs Brooks who were home for the weekend. Despite it being a dry but chilly day, they decided to walk to church as the master's health had improved.

After the service, the congregation chatted in the churchyard, and the various household servants formed little clusters until it was time to go home. Lunch was a cold buffet prepared by Mrs Brooks, and they would have dinner later that evening. Once they had eaten and the dining room cleared, Mary settled with her father in the drawing room to catch up on her progress at boarding school and talk about Jane's good news.

In the kitchen, Cassie could not wait to leave as soon as Mrs Brooks gave her the word. "Right, my girl," said Mrs Brooks. "I expect you want to be off to see that young man of yours?"

"Yes, please, Mrs Brooks," replied Cassie, looking smart in her Sunday best coat and scarf. She knew Isaac would be waiting for her in a cab just down the road.

"Right, well off you go. Be a good girl, and keep your hand on your tuppence," Mrs Brooks added. Cassie knew exactly what Mrs Brooks meant, and felt herself blush, as she hurried out the door.

As Cassie climbed up beside Isaac, he delicately placed a rug across her knees, and they set off towards The Downs. A cool breeze swept across their faces as they rode. "I have some sandwiches, my luvver, and some bottles of that ginger ale that you like. Now give us a kiss." he said, smiling.

"You're wicked, you are," said Cassie, pretending to pull away as Isaac leaned forward to kiss her. "Someone might see us."

"I don't care," said Isaac. "I love you; you know."

Before Cassie could even think about it, she blurted out, "I love you, too." She realised, for the first time, that what she had said was true. There was a brief silence as Isaac registered the words that Cassie had uttered.

Mrs Brooks watched the young couple from the window as they rode away. From what she had heard and seen of Isaac, Cassie could be a lucky young girl, but it was early days. She had become fond of Cassie and did not want to see her hurt. Mrs Brooks began to hatch a little plan, and the family party in a couple of weeks' time would be the perfect opportunity to put it into action.

Trying to remain casual, even though his heart was pounding, Isaac suggested, "Let's go around the Downs, stop, and have our sandwiches, then go to my house for tea, and I promise to get you home before six o'clock so Mrs Brooks doesn't have a fit. My Da said he likes you very much, and he said you remind him of my Ma when she was young... and..." Isaac hesitated before blurting out, "I have told him I am going to marry you, if you will have me. What do you say to that then? Not for a year, mind, as I must save up a bit more."

Cassie's head was swimming with happiness: she had never felt anything like it in her life. "Of course, I will marry you, but you will have to ask my Da and Ma first, and I don't know what Mrs Brooks will say!"

"Right, that's it then, we will see them next Sunday without fail."

Cheese sandwiches and ginger ale had never tasted so good.

After a light tea later that afternoon, Isaac confirmed his intentions to his father, who had taken to Cassie the moment he saw her and thought she would make a good wife for his son. Isaac was as good as his word and returned Cassie to Redland in plenty of time. As he gently kissed her goodnight, he took a little box from his waistcoat and gave it to her.

"Just something to celebrate today and making me the happiest man in Bristol," said Isaac. Cassie opened the box and inside was a little beautifully engraved floral locket.

"It's real silver," said Isaac, "but one day it will be gold, and when it's all official, I will get you an engagement ring, just to say you're mine."

Tears welled up in Cassie's eyes. "I love it and will wear it forever," she declared. "I have never had anything so lovely before." She kissed Isaac and ran towards the house.

Breathless and excited, Cassie rushed into the kitchen where Mrs Brooks was busy peeling vegetables for dinner. After sitting down at the large kitchen table to catch her breath, Mrs Brooks asked, "Well, my girl. What have you been up to?"

Cassie could not contain herself any longer and blurted out, "I'm getting married!" Mrs Brooks stopped what she was doing and looked straight at Cassie, surprised by the news. "Are you saying what I thought you said, young Cassie?" she asked.

Cassie confirmed her news and explained that Isaac had asked her to marry him. "Next weekend he's going to ask my Ma and Pa. I said yes," Cassie added nervously.

Anticipating possible anger from Mrs Brooks, Cassie was relieved when she received a warm response. Mrs Brooks stood up, walked over to Cassie with her arms stretched out, and gave her a big hug. "You lucky, lucky girl," she exclaimed. Mrs Brooks had been planning to talk to Isaac during the party and ask him about his intentions towards Cassie. But now that the news was out, she was pleased with the outcome.

Cassie explained that the wedding would not be for another year, as Isaac had to save up, and she would just be 19. Mrs Brooks hugged her again and said, "Now, go and get your best clothes off and come down straight away. We have dinner to serve, and it's getting late."

As Cassie left to get changed, Mrs Brooks could not help but feel a little sad. She had spent so much time training and helping Cassie, and now that she was getting married, she would have to leave. But at the same time, Mrs Brooks was proud of Cassie for being sensible and mature about her future.

With dinner ready, they all sat down to eat. Mrs Brooks had prepared a light vegetable soup as a starter, accompanied by some small bread rolls. The beef joint was almost ready and would have to rest while the vegetables cooked, and a gravy made from the juices. For dessert, they had a strawberry jelly that Mrs Brooks had made that morning, which she had placed on the cold slab in the pantry, hoping it would set in time.

As they ate, Cassie could not help but feel grateful for all the advice and training Mrs Brooks had given her over the past four years. She knew that she would not be where she was today without her. And as for Mrs Brooks, she was already thinking about who she could train next to help with the household chores. But for now, she was simply happy to enjoy the moment and would perhaps treat herself to a new frock for the wedding.

Chapter 24

B ack in Portland Square Jane was feeling well and the household was running smoothly, but she knew that they needed to hire a housemaid come chambermaid. William had suggested looking into agencies that specialised in recommending servants for private households, so she spoke to Isabella and Pamela about her intention to do so. Isabella felt flattered to be asked to join Jane and Mrs Brooks for the interviews, as servants were not typically consulted on these matters.

A couple of days later, Henry visited and explained that Isabella and Pamela had come from his personal contacts, but he knew of no one at the moment. However, he had made some enquiries and suggested that William contact an agency in Old Market[10] that specialised in recommending servants for private households. Henry also hinted that he might be bringing a young lady with him to the upcoming party, but he would not say anything more. Jane could not resist teasing him as he left, calling him a dark horse.

The following evening, William visited the agency that Henry had recommended. The doors to its offices led upstairs to a large room surrounded by tall wooden cabinets and an imposing desk with a slightly smaller one behind. As William entered the room, a gentleman rose from behind the desk and introduced himself as Mr Charles Stevinson, sole proprietor of Stevinson and Boucher, Domestic Servants to the Gentry.

---

10. An area outside the medieval Bristol castle that supplied the people of the city with fresh produce and goods. The stag and hounds pub' (still standing) was the original site of the 'pie poundre court' whose purpose was to administer swift justice for any crimes committed on market and fair days.

William handed Mr Stevinson one of his business cards and explained that they had recently moved into Portland Square and were looking for an additional servant, a lady's maid. Mr Stevinson said that they had come to the right establishment, as they prided themselves on the quality of their servants who had served some of the finest households in the city.

Mr Stevinson asked his clerk, Braddick, to bring him the files in the B cabinet, as he was sure they had several suitable candidates whose details William might care to look at. Braddick quickly produced a file from the cabinet marked with a bold B, and Mr Stevinson handed it to William for his consideration.

"Please take a seat, sir, and peruse these. I am sure you will find some suitable candidates that will suit your household," assured Mr Stevinson. After a quick look through the file, William noticed that all the girls had references and previous experience. He looked up to Mr Stevinson, who was leaning forward towards William with a friendly smile, anxiously awaiting his words. "They all look well qualified," said William. "But it is my wife who will make the final decision." Mr Stevinson raised his eyebrows slightly. William added, "Do you think you could choose three and send them to this address on Friday morning, say after 10 o'clock please?"

"Certainly, sir, and I am sure you will be happy with the selection. Now, sir, our terms: if you select someone from our service, we ask for one month's wages in advance. Do you find that acceptable?"

"Perfectly," said William and shook hands with Mr Stevinson before bidding him farewell.

William arrived home a bit later than usual and explained to Jane about his visit. Friday would give Jane plenty of time to contact Mrs Brooks, and in fact, she might pay a visit tomorrow and see her father and ask if he would mind if Grace could help.

The following day, Jane arrived by cab at Redland and Cassie answered the door. She smiled and ushered Jane into the hallway and took her hat, coat, and gloves before showing her into the study where her father was reading the *Bristol Times*. Her father looked up with surprise. "How lovely to see you, Jane. We were not expecting you today. I will ring for Mrs Brooks to get us some tea."

"Actually, father, it was Grace I have come to see you about. I wonder if you could spare her for a couple of hours on Friday as I must interview for a new housemaid. I could do with her experience."

"Of course, my dear, that goes without saying. She is in the kitchen. While you are there perhaps you could also request some of her famous fruitcake," her father replied.

Jane made her way to the kitchen where Mrs Brooks and Cassie were busy with chores. "Ahh, Miss Jane, this is a lovely surprise, I must say. I do miss you so much not living here anymore."

"Yes, I miss you too, Grace. I wondered if I might ask you to do me a little favour and help me again do some interviews on Friday. I have spoken to father, and he is quite happy if you are?"

"Of course, my dear. I would love to. And now, I must tell you our news! Young Cassie here is getting married. What do you think of that?" Before Jane could respond, Mrs Brooks continued, "You know him, the coachman, Isaac, a nice, honourable young man."

Jane said, "Oh my, how wonderful," turning to Cassie. "When is the big day?" she asked.

"Not for a year," said Mrs Brooks. "They're being very sensible, aren't you, my girl?"

Jane went over to Cassie and placed her hand on hers and said, 'Congratulations!,' to which Cassie spluttered, "Thank you, madame."

"Now," said Jane, "how about some tea, and is there any of your fruitcake, Grace? I know we would all love some, including father."

On Friday, a cab arrived to take Mrs Brooks to Portland Square, which she considered a little treat since it was something she could seldom afford. She enjoyed the ride, which took about half an hour, and soon arrived at the grand terraced Georgian house. The cab driver helped her down and she rang the bell of the black painted door with highly polished brass that looked like gold.

Pamela answered the door and immediately recognised Mrs Brooks as the lady who had interviewed her with the Mistress. She curtsied, smiled, and took Mrs Brooks' hat and coat before showing her into the drawing room. Pamela knocked on the door and announced Mrs Brooks, who momentarily felt quite important.

Jane was waiting in the drawing room and seated in the middle of three chairs that had been placed near the large window, with a roaring fire in the ornate cast iron fireplace. Jane rose and gave Grace a big hug and a kiss on the cheek, thanking her for her help.

Jane explained that the agency had sent a messenger with the names of three girls they thought would be suitable for the position. They should arrive at hourly intervals, but in case of overlap, a couple of chairs had been placed in the hallway. All the girls would go to the agency first, and they would send them to the address at appropriate intervals since the girls would probably not have their own timepieces. Jane had also asked Isabella to join them.

The first girl, Daisy Wright, arrived exactly on time. She was a dark-haired, poorly dressed girl with a polite countenance. She was 16 and a half and had been working since she was 13 years old. Her family came from Bedminster, and her father worked in the glassworks. She had worked two jobs in public houses that took in paying guests, where her job was to light the fires, black the grates, make the beds, and clean out the slop buckets. She had no experience in private households, and Mrs Brooks' keen eye noticed that her fingernails were dirty. Isabella and Mrs Brooks asked Daisy some questions, which she answered quite well. Jane thanked her for coming and said they would contact the agency in due course. Daisy curtseyed and left with a feeling that she had not got the position.

The next girl to arrive at the appointed hour was Dolly Perkins, who already worked in a household in Redcliffe. She was 18 and had been employed in the same household since she was nearly 14 and was now a housemaid. Unfortunately, her mistress, who was the daughter and only child remaining at home, was getting married herself, and the master was going to live with his son. All the servants were to be dismissed over the next four months or so, as there were no positions for them in other households. Dolly could read well and had also learned to cook, sew, and iron. She had started as a scullery maid and worked her way up to a housemaid come chambermaid. All three were impressed with Miss Perkins, but the only problem was that she could not take another position for several months.

Jane was in a bit of a quandary. She had already decided to offer Dolly the position of chambermaid, but William needed someone to start immediately. So, Jane asked Dolly if she would not mind waiting in the hallway and promised it would not be for too long. When Mrs Brooks and Isabella agreed that Dolly would be ideal for the position, Jane explained to her, "I would be quite happy to wait, but William insists I have someone now."

Mrs Brooks was the first to speak, "Young Cassie will be leaving within the year, so we will need someone else at Redland. In four or five months when this young girl is free, she could join the household. There would be an overlap, but with Miss Mary leaving boarding school later in the year, it could work out very well. She would be a housemaid and a bit of everything else." Jane thought about what Mrs Brooks said and felt that with Dolly's capabilities, it was worth accommodating her at the Bright household instead.

"Isabella, would you ask her to come in please and we will see what she has to say." Dolly Perkins came into the room looking a bit worried as Jane asked her to sit down. "I am unable to offer you the position in the household, Miss Perkins," said Jane. Dolly's face dropped as she thought this would have been a lovely house to work in. "However, Mrs Brooks will have a position at my father's house in Redland in about four- or five-months' time and would like to offer you the position of general housemaid. What do you think?" Dolly's face lit up, and she confirmed her acceptance. "Excellent," said Jane. "We will notify the agency with all the details and thank you for coming today." Dolly gave a practised curtsey and Isabella showed her out. As Dolly was leaving, Isabella whispered in her ear, "That Mrs Brooks is a lovely lady. I am sure you will love working with her."

"Right," said Jane, "the next is Miss Ellen Drewett, according to the list, but she's not due yet. Shall we have some refreshments? This interviewing is inclined to make you thirsty." Jane rang the small bell that was situated on the table next to her chair and requested some tea and cake. Miss Drewett arrived on time and was a bit older than the previous two at 20 years old. She was a portly young lady, well dressed according to her station in life and with a very friendly smile and of smart appearance. Mrs Brooks and Isabella took to her straight away, and Jane was not far behind as she asked her about her experience.

Ellen sat up straight in her chair and explained that her family came from the Danes Lane area of nearby Keynsham, and she had been the youngest of a family of five. Unfortunately, her mother Mary had died giving birth, so it was her older sisters who had brought her up. As they had gradually all left home to work or get married, she had been left to look after her father at an early age. He had a carter[11] business until he became ill, and it was her duty to look after him. He had died when she was 14, and she had suddenly found herself homeless until one of her sisters, who had married and gone to live in Bristol, had given her a roof over her head. She could read a little, and the most obvious work for her was to be in service, so that is what she did, gaining employment as an assistant cook in a house on Worcester Road in Clifton.

Ellen soon learned the house duties and procedures and was eventually promoted from the kitchen to lady's maid, joining another girl. Her duties were to the two eldest daughters, and she learned very quickly from Maisie, the other maid. She settled in

---

11. The carter might work with a pony and trap to transport goods, especially from the country into the towns on market days.

very well and was praised for her level of competence. She had been happy there ever since.

"What circumstances bring you here today, Miss Drewett?" asked Jane.

"Well, madame, both the ladies have now married and left home, and my services are no longer required, but I do have a reference I can show you." Ellen took the letter from her bag and passed it to Jane. It read:

> *To whom it may concern, Miss Ellen Drewett has given the household excellent service and has been found to be reliable in her duties, diligent, and trustworthy. We are very reluctant to dispense with her services, but our household requirements have now changed. Yours faithfully, Mrs Elisabeth Bell.*

Jane passed the letter to Mrs Brooks, and Isabella in turn. "Would you mind waiting in the hallway for a moment, please, Miss Drewett? Miss Dando will show you out, and I promise not to keep you waiting very long."

"Well," said Jane, after Ellen had left the room, "she is a very likeable young woman, and her reference is excellent. What do you think, Grace?"

"I agree," said Grace, and Isabella nodded.

"Right," said Jane, "so I shall offer her the position. Would you please show her back in, Isabella?" Ellen re-entered the room and took her seat as gestured.

"Miss Drewett," said Jane, "you have an excellent reference, and I would like to offer you the position of lady's maid. I would like an immediate start."

"Yes, thank you so much, madame," Ellen said eagerly. "I can start tomorrow morning."

"Excellent," said Jane. "Isabella is our cook and housekeeper, and she will show you to where your room will be, and we will expect you at 10 o'clock tomorrow morning. If you have any further questions, I am sure Isabella can answer them for you."

Ellen curtseyed again with a broad smile and left the room with Isabella. Jane looked at Grace Brooks and said, "Well, I think we both need a glass of sherry after a good morning's work, and thank you again, Grace. I could not have done it without you. Now, for that sherry."

Isabella took Ellen to the kitchen where Pamela Berry was setting up the light lunch that Isabella had prepared earlier. "You'll like it here," said Pamela. "They're nice people and we all get along. Have a sandwich. There's plenty to go round."

"Are you sure it will be all, right?" asked Ellen.

"Of course, it is," said Pamela. "We don't starve here. Have you seen your bedroom yet?"

"Not yet," said Ellen. "Miss Dando is going to show me in a minute."

"Call me Isabella, but not in front of the master or mistress," said Isabella. "The bedrooms are very comfortable. They overlook the square, we have fireplaces and stone hot water bottles if we need them, and they're not stingy with the food either."

Isabella led Ellen up the stairs and showed her to her room. "Here we are," she said, opening the door. "It is not the biggest room, but it is cosy and has everything you need. And if you need anything else, just let me know."

Ellen stepped inside and looked around. The room was small, but it had a comfortable bed, a chest of drawers, and a wardrobe. A vase of fresh flowers sat on the windowsill, and the curtains drawn back, letting in the afternoon sun. "It's perfect," Ellen said, turning to Isabella. "Thank you so much."

Pamela was right, the rooms were comfortable, and Ellen would miss her previous home, but she was sure she would be happy here. Isabella showed her where all the essentials were, and they went back down to the hallway. "See you tomorrow, and don't be late on your first day," said Isabella.

"I won't. I'm really looking forward to getting settled in and starting my new position tomorrow," replied Ellen.

She could not believe her luck. She had gone from being out of work to having a new position in a beautiful home with friendly people. She felt excited and grateful for this new opportunity.

It had been a very tiring day, so William and Jane had gone to bed early. A few hours after falling asleep William started to scream out, "Help! Help! Murder!" and thrashing his arms about, accidentally hitting Jane on her arm. Both the noise and sensation immediately woke her as she saw her husband was having a nightmare and managed to grab one of William's arms. Jane tried to awaken him gently calling, "William. William! It's Jane. Everything is fine. You're safe at home."

William jolted awake at the sound of Jane's familiar voice. He was sweating and disorientated and hung on to Jane.

"It was all happening again," stammered William. "The attack. It was so real; it was like I was back in Ludlow. I am so sorry my darling."

"You're safe William," reassured Jane. "It was just a bad dream my love. No one can hurt you now."

William held her close, and Jane could feel his body shaking slightly against hers. Jane placed her hand on William's cheek and slowly got out of bed to draw back the curtains and let some moonlight into the room. She also lit the candle by the side of the bed.

There was a faint knock on the door and Isabella's voice called, "Is everything alright Mistress? We heard a cry for help."

"Yes," replied Jane. "Everything is fine, thank you. It was just the master having a bad dream. Please go back to bed."

Jane returned to William and put her arms reassuringly around his torso. It took a while for to fall asleep. William was re-thinking the attack in his head and Jane wondered how long it would take for William to return to normal. It was not the first time he had had such a dream and she worried that it would not be the last.

Eventually they both fell soundly to sleep as the candle continued to burn.

The following morning at breakfast Jane suggested that William might send a message to Dr Barber to ask if he could help. William assured her it would not happen again and there was no reason to bother the doctor. Alas, Jane was still fretting and although she felt as if she was going behind William's back, decided to write a letter to Henry asking his advice.

A few days later Henry called at the house whilst William was still at business and Jane told him exactly what had happened.

"My dear brother has gone through a harrowing time and was lucky to have survived. It is not surprising that his is now suffering such torment and is finding it difficult not to re-live those horrific hours. I agree with you, Jane, that William should seek help from Dr Barber as a matter of urgency. He might at least be able to give William something to ensure a good night's rest."

"Yes," said Jane. "I am sure I can persuade him to see the sense of it, but I wonder if I should wait to see if it happens again and meanwhile not mention it to him." Henry agreed but urged Jane to let him know. Henry rose and kissed Jane on the forehead and left.

Some weeks later William experienced another night terror and Jane sent word to Henry straight away. A few days later Henry called at the house one evening and was shown into William's study by Isabella. William was enjoying a whisky and invited his brother to join him.

"This is pleasant surprise," said William, handing Henry a glass. "I'm delighted to see you. What brings you to this side of town?"

"I must confess, William," said Henry. "I have been worried about you and I know the rest of the family are too. Jane has told me about your problems sleeping."

William, stood up abruptly from his chair nearly spilling his drink as he did so. "It is none of your business Henry." He exploded with rage; his face became red with anger. "How dare you discuss me behind my back?" Henry was quite taken aback by the outburst of his brother which was completely out of character. It was as if he had turned into a completely different person, a stranger, for those few seconds.

As if woken from a trance, William suddenly realised what he had said and felt a wave of both shame and remorse He began to sob, and turned to embrace his brother, asking for his forgiveness.

"Oh Henry. I do not know what comes over me. It is like a dark cloud descends and I am taken back to that dreadful night."

He sat down and held his head in his hands. He felt the relief of having shared his worst fears with his brother. There was silence between them for few moments, as William shook his head and finally said, "I know this situation has not been fair to anyone, myself, Jane, and the whole family. It is time. I will do as Jane suggests. I will call Doctor Barber in the morning."

Henry nodded slowly, relieved at his brother's decision.

Two days later as arranged Dr Barber called and suggested a private meeting with William in his study, but William insisted Jane be present at the consultation. William explained that he had reoccurring memories of the attack on his person in Ludlow, and it seemed so real that he awoke from his sleep in great panic and terror. Jane also explained what was happening to William and his sudden outburst of losing his temper, which was completely against his nature.

Dr Barber listened and made copious notes. He had known the Bright family for many years and had come to know William quite well in a professional sense. Reading through what he had written, he remarked, "The brain is a powerful and strange organ, and we are only just beginning to discover certain scientific facts about it, but there is a great deal we do not understand. I am sure things will improve over a period, but meanwhile I think it important that you sleep and rest well. Talking about these things is often the first step towards resolution. In the meantime, I will give you a potion that will help you to sleep. I want you to take it about half an hour before you retire at night. I will call and see you again in about three weeks' time unless I receive a request from you before. Please ask your maid to call at my house later today and the potion will be ready for you."

William and Jane thanked Dr Barber and he left. They both felt reassured by what he has told them, and William started to take the potion that evening and slept very well with no disturbances apart from feeling a little drowsy in the mornings, to which his body soon became accustomed. Thankfully, the nightmares did not return and during the daytime his nerves were also much improved. He rarely lost his temper and gradually life became settled, and William hoped he could put the past finally behind him.

Chapter 25

At the Mackreth household in Clifton, everyone was busy preparing for George's return from London to attend the family party. Mary was particularly excited, and Henry was planning a little surprise. Bridget, the housekeeper, had noticed a change in Henry's behaviour. He was more secretive about his movements, and in a lighter mood with a new spring in his step.

Bridget guessed that a young lady was involved, and she was not wrong. That evening, after dinner, the family gathered in the drawing room when Henry announced that he would be bringing someone home after church on Sunday. Despite his elder brother George's encouragement to play a guessing game, Henry kept his cards close to his chest. "I am saying nothing more," he said. "You will have to wait."

Mary conjectured that William might know his brother's secret but if he did, he gave nothing away. Meanwhile Henry remained tight-lipped. "Wait and see, young lady," he said. "But I expect you to be on your best behaviour, if that's possible."

On Sunday, the family attended church as usual, but instead of returning home for lunch, Henry hailed a cab, promising not to be too long. Little did they know, he was off to the vicarage of the Reverend James Fouracres, his wife Lillian, and their only daughter, Anne.

Henry had met Anne when he visited the Reverend Fouracres during the preparations for Jane and William's wedding. He was immediately attracted to her. She was almost as tall as Henry, with blonde hair, a fair complexion, and sparkling blue eyes. He could not stop staring at her. Henry had made excuses to call and see the Reverend Fouracres with every trivial excuse, hoping to see Anne. His attentions had not gone unnoticed by the Reverend and his wife. They were secretly pleased and happy to encourage the situation. Their daughter was also enamoured with this young man who came from a well-respected family and had good prospects with his family's business.

Henry eventually asked for permission to call on Anne, and they willingly gave their consent. At first, her mother acted as a chaperone, but now they were allowed to go out on Saturday or Sunday afternoons, weather permitting, by themselves.

Today was the big day for Henry to introduce Anne to his family. He had covertly managed to ask Great-Aunt Charlotte and Uncle Charles for permission to bring Anne to the party. Both were delighted for young Henry. This was the first time they had heard of Henry's blossoming romance and were looking forward to meeting the young lady. "Two family surprises," thought Charlotte, who could hardly contain her excitement as the hostess.

The Reverend Fouracres and his wife had agreed to the plan, and soon Henry and Anne were on their way to the Mackreth residence in Clifton in time for lunch. In the carriage, Henry could not keep his eyes off Anne. She looked so pretty in a pale lavender-coloured dress and matching bonnet, with her blonde curly hair framing her face.

"Henry," exclaimed Anne. "Why do you keep looking at me like that?" Henry reached out and held her gloved hand in his, looking straight into her pale blue eyes. He whispered, so the cabby could not hear, "It's because I think you are the most beautiful woman I have ever seen, and I love you." Anne felt the colour rise in her cheeks as she reddened and whispered back to Henry, "I love you too, Henry Mackreth."

"Will you marry me, Anne?"

"Of course I will Henry." She responded without hesitation. Henry kissed her gently on the cheek and after a few moments

Anne added, "you must speak to Papa to ask his permission." Henry nodded and continued to gaze into her eyes.

Within half an hour, they arrived at their destination, and Henry helped Anne down from the cab and rang the bell. Florence answered the door with an open-mouthed look of amazement and a slightly wobbly curtsey. She had never seen Henry with any female outside the family before. "This is Miss Fouracres," said Henry proudly, as Florence offered to take her cape, hat, and gloves. "I hope we are still in time for lunch. We have another guest. Can you please inform Bridget?"

Florence curtseyed and rushed off to the kitchen. Meanwhile, Henry escorted Anne into the drawing room, where everyone was chatting away. There was a brief hush as they all looked up when Henry and Anne entered. At first, there was some curiosity and surprise, followed by smiles from everyone.

"May I introduce Miss Anne Fouracres, the Reverend Fouracres' daughter, the lady I one day hope to marry." There was a chorus of applause and congratulations at Henry's news as he then formally introduced Anne to his father, who had stood up and clasped Anne's hand. "It's a great pleasure to meet you, my dear. We knew Henry was up to something, but this is a great surprise." It was then siblings George and Mary's turn. George took Anne's hand and said, "You are Henry's little secret. We wondered where he'd been spending all his time lately." Mary was a little more shy, and said nervously, "I am very pleased to meet you." Anne was blushing from head to foot and was holding Henry's hand as tightly as possible as she greeted all the close family.

"I remember your father from William and Jane's wedding," said John. "I am looking forward to meeting him and your mother. When do you think that might be?"

"Next Saturday," replied Henry before Anne had a chance to answer. "It's all arranged with Great-Aunt Charlotte. She is sending invitations to Anne's mother and father, and we will all arrive together, quite possibly with William and Jane. This is all such marvellous news."

William Snr was about to ring the bell and ask about lunch when the door was knocked, and Bridget announced that the food was ready. "Excellent," said Henry. "I could eat a horse."

The following Tuesday afternoon, Henry called into Christopher George and Co to tell William about Anne and wondered if he could bring her to dinner one evening to introduce her to him and Jane before the party Saturday. "Well!" exclaimed William. "You old dog! You kept that well-hidden, I must say. Of course, you can come to dinner. How about tomorrow evening? Jane will be thrilled, and so am I. I can't wait to meet your future fiancée."

"Yes, not quite yet," said Henry. "I've still got to ask her father's permission."

"Of course, that goes without saying. You must not jump the gun and follow the correct protocol," replied William, giving his brother a hug. "I am delighted for you and look forward to tomorrow evening."

Chapter 26

The day of the party soon arrived, and Henry planned to pick up Anne and her family from the vicarage before heading to William and Jane's in Portland Square. He arrived there in plenty of time, knowing that he had an especially important question to ask the Reverend Fouracres. The maid answered the door and showed him directly into the parlour where the Reverend James Fouracres was waiting.

"Good evening, Henry," said the vicar with his usual bright and cheery countenance. "The ladies are still getting ready, I'm afraid. You cannot rush them."

"Sir," said Henry, feeling a little bit sick. "There is something I wish to ask you."

"Really, young man? And what is that?" the vicar asked.

"I love and wish to marry your daughter, sir."

The vicar paused, inwardly smiled, and said, "And what does my daughter think about that?" holding Henry's gaze.

"I am sure she is very agreeable, sir, and I know she loves me too," said Henry, his voice becoming quieter and quieter.

At this point, the two were interrupted by Mrs Fouracres and Anne, both looking very pretty in their gowns and capes. It was the first time Henry had noticed how handsome Mrs Lillian Fouracres was for her age. Like mother like daughter, thought Henry.

"Lillian," said the casual Reverend Fouracres, "this young man has asked for our daughter's hand in marriage. I have no objection. Do you, my dear?"

Lillian Fouracres's face was beaming as she replied that she had no objection at all if her daughter was happy. Both looked at Anne as she rushed to her parents and put her arms around them.

"Mama, Papa! I love Henry so much and want to marry him more than anything."

Turning towards Henry, the Reverend Fouracres declared with a broad grin, "There you are, young Henry, you have your answer. God bless you both, and I hope your family is as pleased as we are."

Henry looked slightly embarrassed, as if he had realised that the Reverend Fouracres may have suspected that they already knew. "They love her as much as I do already, sir. That is settled then. Let us all go to the party."

Within ten minutes, they were in Portland Square where William and Jane were waiting, and the carriage was soon rumbling over the cobbles to the grandeur of Queen's Square. As they arrived at Great-Aunt Charlotte and Uncle Charles's house, they could see beacons lit on either side of the gate columns, and the private carriages had been taken into the stables area or parked adjacent to the grass areas of the square. There were footmen at the door and inside to take the guests' coats, gloves, hats, and other items. All the guests were then individually announced by the senior butler as they entered the large reception room.

William and Jane's family had already arrived and were socialising with all the family members, comprising a selection of cousins, aunts, and uncles who generally only met up on special family occasions. Great-Aunt Charlotte was in her element and seemed to float like a majestic butterfly from one family member to the next. She suddenly spotted William and Jane and the Mackreth entourage and drew away rather too swiftly from a distant cousin with whom she was in mid-conversation. With much fanfare, Great-Aunt Charlotte gave Jane and William a dramatic kiss on their cheeks and congratulated them on the forthcoming happy event, before pirouetting, as if on wheels, towards the Reverend Fouracres, his wife Lillian, and daughter Anne.

Great-Aunt Charlotte commented that she remembered Reverend Fouracres from the wedding and complimented him on his service, which she had thoroughly enjoyed. There was no reason not to believe her, as both Great-Aunt Charlotte and Uncle Charles always spoke their minds. She then turned to Anne, who was holding Henry's hand in a vice-like grip. Anne managed to smile and control the tone of her voice, even though she was hoping the ground would swallow her up. She felt overwhelmed by the number of people and being the centre of attention.

"It is lovely to meet you, Miss Fouracres. You are a very pretty young lady, and Henry is incredibly lucky. You must announce your engagement this evening to all the family. I insist. We have plenty of champagne, and it will be wonderful. But leave it until after dinner when Charles and I can garner everyone's attention. Meanwhile, enjoy yourselves, and dinner will be served in about half an hour."

The family continued to mingle and catch up with each other's news. The news of William and Jane's expected 'happy event' had leaked out, with cries of delight and well-wishing, which would really make Great-Aunt Charlotte's announcement void. But, of course, no one would ever dream of telling her it was unnecessary.

The guests were ushered into the large dining room beautifully lit by a central chandelier and lights on free-standing columns. The banquet was sumptuous, and no expense spared. The guests were served by liveried footmen, and the wine flowed. The air was filled with laughter and chatter, and everyone was having a glorious time, particularly Great-Aunt Charlotte and Uncle Charles who were both anticipating the joyful announcements they would have the honour of making to their receptive guests. These events gave them the greatest pleasure, the pleasure of seeing everyone entertained and content.

After dinner, everyone retired to the reception room, where a pianist had been engaged to play for the rest of the evening. The footmen soon arrived with silver trays filled with glasses of chilled champagne, and Great-Aunt Charlotte and Uncle Charles took centre stage. The room fell silent, and the speeches began.

By 11, the party started to leave for their private and hired carriages. Kisses, handshakes, and sincere words of thanks were exchanged with Great-Aunt Charlotte and Uncle Charles, both beaming with pride as everyone disappeared into the damp Bristol night.

Chapter 27

Now Henry and Anne were now officially engaged, Anne proudly wore a beautiful diamond ring. The wedding was planned for the following July, and by then, 'God willing,' Jane and William's baby would have arrived, and the dreaded Shrewsbury Trial would be finished. It would be a new beginning for them all. Christmas would soon be here, and everyone was excited at the prospect of this joyful time but also thought of the not-so-fortunate. Both the Mackreth and Bright families always made generous donations to the church to be given to the extremely poor.

This year was going to be slightly different as Prince Albert had introduced the German tradition of bringing a fir tree into the household and decorating it with glass baubles or anything bright and colourful. William had also heard of the practice from America and thought it would add extra fun to the Christmas activities. In the Mackreth household, they always bought ivy at Christmas from the market and added coloured paper flowers and cotton wool to it, festooning the picture rails and staircase. Goose and beef would be on the menu this year, and of course, the plum puddings that Bridget had made months ago.

There was certainly plenty to do, as it would be William and Jane's first Christmas as a married couple. They needed to purchase presents for both their family and their servants and order all the necessary food ahead of time. The staff would traditionally have Boxing Day off, but some whose families lived too far away would continue as usual. William thought it was unfair for Pamela, who could not travel to her family home, and spoke to Jane about how they could make it up to her.

All their servants had been proving to be very efficient and dependable, and the Mackreths wanted to show their appreciation. The days leading up to Christmas flew by, with William busy at the foundry and Jane ordering and buying presents to make sure no one was left out. The cider, wine, spices, and other goods had all arrived, and the Christmas tree had come with instructions on how to set it up, from the jolly purveyor of Frenchay village on the outskirts of Bristol.

Isabella and Pamela brought the tree into the drawing room, and Jane supervised its placement near the window. The tree was about five feet tall, and there was great excitement as Isabella held it straight while Pamela shovelled in the sand to keep it upright. The smell of the pine tree was lovely, and tomorrow they would tie on small oranges studded with cloves, which gave off a wonderful aroma. Golden paper had been bought to cut out stars, and little netted bags were to be filled with nuts and sweetmeats. Jane thought the cotton wool looked good on the ivy, so she tried some on the tree. The Christmas tradition would never be quite the same again.

When Christmas Day finally arrived, all the preparation ensured that everything went like clockwork. Christmas dinner was served promptly at 1 o'clock, and the dining room looked beautiful with its table decorations and lit candelabra. The servants would eat the same as William and Jane, and William gave Isabella permission to offer everyone a glass of port each.

After the table was cleared and Isabella was congratulated on a beautifully cooked Christmas dinner, William asked her to bring Ellen and Pamela into the drawing room. Pamela seemed a bit wobbly on her feet, but soon recovered. William wished them all a happy Christmas and gave them small presents from him and Jane. They were all amazed as William handed each a small package, and each servant opened a pretty lace-edged handkerchief. Ellen and Isabella had also been given a little silver brooch each in the shape of leaves, and Pamela a pair of silver-hooped earrings. Pamela was quite shocked and emotional, saying she had never been given anything so nice before.

Back in the drawing room, William gave Jane a delicately pink-wrapped gift, and inside was a single string of pearls. Jane exclaimed that they were exquisite and asked William to help her put them on. After fastening them around her neck, Jane rushed over to the mirror to see their beauty and elegance reflected back at her. She turned to give William a kiss and said, "Now it's your turn, my darling."

Jane reached up to one of the higher branches of the tree and passed a small green and black package to William. He looked at Jane quizzically as he carefully opened it, not having a clue what it might be. Removing the paper revealed a black felt-covered hinged box. The sprung box flipped open, and a solid gold half hunter watch gleamed back at him.

"I love it," said William. "And I will keep it for special occasions." William pulled Jane towards him and kissed her until it almost took her breath away. "I truly am the most fortunate man to have been blessed with such a thoughtful and beautiful wife. This Christmas with just the two of us has been the best ever."

On Boxing Day, the servants made an early start to see their respective families, and a cab had been hired to take William and Jane to the family gathering at the Bright Home in Redland.

Both the Mackreths and Brights would be together again. Young Mary and Joseph would be home, and Mrs Brooks, who was seeing an old friend later in the day, had prepared a beef and dumpling stew, one of her specialities, so it could easily be kept hot without spoiling. William's brother George was also home from London and surprised the family by announcing he would be moving back to Bristol, which everyone was delighted about. Both the young Marys were simply excited and chatted constantly without drawing breath. Henry was there with his fiancée Anne, and Eleanor with her husband, who was a man of few words. Young Joseph was being asked about his apprenticeship, which was demanding work but very enjoyable. He still had three years to go before he would qualify as an accountant like his brother-in-law, William. The day was full of lively conversation, revelry, and games, and went on late into the evening when the Mackreths and William and Jane finally left to go to their respective homes.

The ringing in of the New Year was welcomed, but it also provided a stark reminder for both William and Henry that they would need to start thinking about the forthcoming trial in Shrewsbury and the travel arrangements they would have to make.

Part Two

Chapter 1

Everyone prayed that 1841 would be a happier year for everyone. William and Jane would be having their first child, Henry and Anne would be getting married, and young Cassie would hopefully find her happiness by tying the knot with her Isaac.

The best inn in Shrewsbury was ironically the Unicorn Inn where the whole sorry saga had begun and was where Henry and William had decided to stay during the trial. William promptly wrote to Mr Goodwin, the landlord, requesting rooms for himself and Henry from the 22nd of March for an open period. No one could predict how long the trial would last.

Within a week, William received a reply from a delighted Mr Goodwin, confirming the reservation of two of his best rooms and assuring William and Henry of their undivided service and attention. As soon as the letter arrived, Mrs Goodwin had recognised William's name from the newspapers of the previous year. Everyone in town was eagerly anticipating the trial. She had pointed out to her husband that it would be particularly good for business. The couple themselves had also been requested to give evidence.

As March arrived, William and Henry made all the necessary preparations. Business commitments were tied up at Christopher George and Co, and Henry did the same in the family business, helped by the fact that their brother George had returned to Bristol.

On a dull, chilly morning, Henry picked William up in the cab that he had travelled in from the family home in Clifton. Both had already said their tearful goodbyes to Jane and Anne and were now at Corn Street to catch the Mail coach. It was busy as usual, and Henry soon spotted young Isaac in the cab line-up, touting for business, and looking very smart alongside his gleaming cab and well-groomed horses.

"That young man deserves to do well," said Henry, pointing out Isaac to his brother. William agreed, thinking of young Cassie.

The coach arrived on time, and they were soon on their way in what was now a familiar journey to them both. They were accompanied by the usual mix of male passengers, soon lulled into a doze by the hypnotic sway of the carriage, only to be routinely awoken by the post horn on their arrival at their scheduled stops.

When they arrived at Shrewsbury in the early evening, they were greeted with great fanfare by Mr Goodwin, his good lady, and servants. They were shown to their adjoining rooms, which were towards the back of the inn, away from the hustle and bustle of the main road. Mr Goodwin repeated that they were undoubtedly their best rooms. As Mr Goodwin turned to leave, he announced, "We have roast beef and lamb on the menu tonight, gentlemen, with an excellent house porter. It will be served in the Commercial Room from half past six, if you would care to join us?"

At dinner, William and Henry were served by the buxom Polly, the maid who had given Josiah Mister the information he was after regarding Mr Ludlow the previous year. She did not recognise the two handsome gentlemen, and they paid her little attention as they were in deep conversation.

The following day, Tuesday the 23rd of March, William and Henry arrived early at the courthouse. The square at the court of assizes next to the Market Hall was packed with thousands of townsfolk and strangers, with many jostling to gain entry to the public gallery.

To their surprise, they noticed that a significant number of women were also present in the crowd. Most of the public in the gallery were women whose husbands were in business or wealthy. Ordinary folks were too busy making a living to survive and could not afford the luxury of being away from their work.

Upon presenting themselves to the clerk of the court, they learned that Sir John Baron Gurney would be the presiding judge and that a Mr Valentine F Lee, a prominent barrister from Oxford, was representing the defendant, while Sergeant-in-Law Mr Fairchild, Mr Godson, and Mr Neale were for the prosecution.

The clerk informed them that he had no idea when William would be called, as there was a lengthy list of witnesses. Inside the courtroom, the standing-room-only gallery was also mainly filled with women. As they waited for something to happen, a hunched figure was brought up from the cells below, causing a loud murmur to echo around the courtroom. People pointed towards the accused, Mr Josiah Mister, prompting a call for silence and "All rise,' by the clerk.

Sir John Baron Gurney then entered the chamber, looking the epitome of authority in his gown and wig. The clerk, the prosecution and defence teams shuffled through mountains of papers on the desks in front of them before satisfying themselves that everything was in order.

The prisoner was then asked to stand, and it was noted that he was smartly dressed as a gentleman wearing a green coat with a velvet collar, a dark satin waistcoat, white shirt, and light-coloured trousers with a dark stripe down the sides. He wore white stockings and black buckled shoes. His dark hair was parted down the middle and smoothed down both sides. He was shaven and would be described as of light build.

The charges were read out as follows, "That on the 20th of August 1840 at the Angel Inn in the town of Ludlow, in the early hours of the morning soon after 4 o'clock, the victim Mr William Mackreth was awakened out of his sleep and found himself severely wounded. There was no doubt that the victim had been feloniously assaulted and wounded by some person.... the prisoner, Mr Josiah Mister that we see before us who is charged with wounding with intent to disfigure, maim and murder. How do you plead Sir? Guilty or not guilty?"

"Not guilty," stated Mister in a loud, precise, and defiant voice, which resulted in another loud murmur from the assembled crowd.

"You may now sit, sir," said the clerk of the court in a very brusque and dismissive manner. Addressing the court, the clerk continued, "By means of an introduction I will now give you a brief summary of what occurred. It is necessary to take you back to some transactions that took place before the incident at Ludlow. The prisoner at the bar was in Shrewsbury on the 12th of August, having ascertained that a person by the name of Mr S Ludlow, a cattle-dealer from Birmingham, would be at the Shrewsbury Fair. It was also common knowledge that Mr Ludlow was known to carry a large amount of money to pay for his purchases from local farmers. The accused further ascertained that Mr Ludlow would be staying at the Unicorn Inn in Shrewsbury and also discovered what bedroom he usually slept in. On this occasion the inn was fully booked, and Mr Ludlow had to share his accommodation with an acquaintance named Mr Jobson.

On August 19th, it has also been established that the accused, Josiah Mister followed, on foot, the same Mr Ludlow to the city of Ludlow. There, Josiah Mister was seen at the town bridge where men were fishing. He enquired about the arrival time of the Red Rover coach from Shrewsbury. When the coach arrived, the prisoner rushed to see Mr Ludlow descend from the coach and followed him into the Commercial Room of the Angel Inn, so closely that the people of the Inn thought they were travelling companions. Mr Ludlow recognised Mister and struck up a conversation with him, remarking, 'You are the young man I saw at Shrewsbury, are you not?'

Meanwhile, the victim, Mr William Miller Mackreth, was already staying at the Angel Inn, travelling for the firm of Christopher George and Co, Bristol. He was also in the Commercial Room at the time, leaving later in the evening and not returning until 10 o'clock. Later that night, the prisoner retired to his room, accompanied by the chambermaid, who showed him the way with a light.

Number 20 was the room assigned to the prisoner, while Number 17 was the room usually occupied by Mr S Ludlow. However, on this night, Number 17 had already been allocated to Mr William Miller Mackreth due to the busy time of the year. Number 17 was the room at the top of the stairs with a passage leading to the prisoner's bedroom, Number 20.

About half an hour after the chambermaid conducted Mr Mackreth to his bedroom, which he locked behind him, she noticed that the door of the prisoner's bedroom (Number 20) was not quite closed, and the candlelight was showing. It has been deduced that whoever committed this act was already concealed in Mr Mackreth's room. This was further supported by the fact that no force was used to break open the door, and no entry was made by the window to Mr Mackreth's room. It was therefore impossible for a person to have entered the room after it was locked, and that the person was already concealed. Witnesses subsequently reported clear and palpable marks in the dust under the bed of a figure. In the early morning, at about four o'clock, Mr Mackreth was suddenly awakened, and the situation in which he found himself was too dreadful to contemplate. His throat was cut from ear to ear through his mouth, and his face had fallen in, along with further injuries."

At this point one of the ladies in the front row of the courtroom fainted and had to be supported by the ladies on either side.

"There was a great dispersal of blood everywhere, and the victim struggled out of bed on the right side nearest to the window. In doing so, he was pulled backwards by someone on his right, tearing his shirt in the process. The medical professionals who examined the victim expressed the expert opinion that the wounds were inflicted by cuts drawn from the right towards the left side of the victim's face. Despite the great loss of blood, the victim was still able to speak and keep his presence of mind. He did not at any time claim to have recognised the person who had committed this act. It will be up to the jury, once they hear all the evidence, to conclude whether the prisoner is guilty or not," explained the clerk of the court.

He continued, "As the victim tried to pull himself away from his attacker, he made a desperate rush for the window. Unable to push up the sash window, he smashed his hand through the glass and managed to utter, "Fire," repeating the word in an effort to make himself heard. Hearing someone leaving the room, he followed in that direction as the light began to filter into the room. He found the door unlocked, opened it, and turned left down the stairs. The landlord and the boot boy, who were in the room just off the bottom of the stairs, were the first to see Mr Mackreth. Their initial impression was that he had tried to harm himself as they assisted him back up to his bedroom.

By this time everyone in the house was stirring and coming out of their rooms to see what all the commotion was about including a curious neighbour to the Angel Inn, a Mr Peach. Fortunately, a surgeon by the name of Mr Crawford, along with one of his assistants, was staying at the inn that night and immediately administered medical aid to the victim. Ink, paper, and a pen were also offered to Mr Mackreth, who was unable to speak and managed to write, "Someone has tried to murder me."

There was a gasp from all in the room, which was now quite crowded by guests, inn staff, and neighbours all trying to catch a glimpse of Mr Mackreth's injuries. The constables were immediately sent for, and a police officer by the name of Hammond was soon on the scene, closely followed by Sergeant Otley and Officer Evans. The horrific events of the night were related to the officers, and Officer Evans was dispatched to awaken the magistrates. Half the town of Ludlow was now awake."

The clerk of the court then summarised what had been given to the magistrates in Ludlow and then forwarded to him at the Shrewsbury assizes. He then explained that further evidence had been gathered, and that witnesses would be called. It would now be up to the prosecution and the defence to cross-examine the witnesses and present their case.

Chapter 2

The heaving courtroom in Shrewsbury had fallen silent to hear the counsel for the prosecution outline its evidence. The prosecution team was made up of three of the top legal minds in the country and would call no less than 40 witnesses to the stand. They were determined to prove that Josiah Mister was the man who had committed this terrible crime and should hang.

The first witness to take the stand was a Mrs Elspeth Goodwin, the landlady of the Unicorn Inn in Shrewsbury. Mr Fairchild, acting for the prosecution, asked if she recognised the defendant. Mrs Goodwin confirmed that she did and added that he owed her money that she wanted to be paid. Mrs Goodwin was a robust lady and well-equipped to handle unruly patrons at the inn, while her husband was quite the opposite and looked like a modest wind might knock him over. Yet despite their differences, the couple were fond of each other.

The judge, Sir John Baron Gurney, reminded the witness to only answer the questions asked of her and not provide any additional information. Mrs Goodwin felt her stomach knot with fear and meekly replied, "Yes, sir."

When asked about the events of Monday, August 10th of the previous year, Mrs Goodwin recounted how the defendant had arrived without a reservation and with only a small carpet bag. She gave him a room because he appeared by the cut of his cloth to be a dressed as a gentleman. However, when it came time to pay for the Farmer's Ordinary and drinks, he claimed he had no money and produced an acceptance[1] for £10, drawn at Leominster and made payable to a Mr Collins on order. Her husband refused to cash the draft, and it later turned out to be fraudulent. The defendant promised to pay the following day but left early in the morning without settling his bill of £1 15s 10d, leaving some of his clothing behind.

The sergeant-in-law thanked Mrs Goodwin before the calling of the next witness, Polly Wiggins, a chambermaid at the Unicorn Inn, who had also served William and Henry the night before. Mr Fairchild asked her to identify herself and her employment and if she recognised the defendant. Polly looked at Mister, with his coal-black eyes that made her shiver and confirmed that he stayed at the inn but left without paying. Sir John reminded Polly to answer only the questions asked of her and asked how she knew the defendant. Polly replied that he had asked her many questions, about a regular customer named Mr Ludlow, whom she saw him speaking with in the Commercial Room.

Mr Fairchild asked, "What was the nature of the questions?"

"He asked me if Mr Ludlow stayed there often and what bedroom he normally stayed in," replied the witness. "I said that he had stayed many times on fair days, at Christmas, and during the summer and usually stayed in the same room. But on this occasion, he was sharing with a friend."

After the witness finished, Mr Fairchild walked away without saying anything more. The next witness called was a Mr Hence, an auctioneer from Ludlow, who had seen and spoken with the prisoner at Cook's farm in Bibury the day after he left Shrewsbury. Mr Cook, a charitable man, had given him some bread, cheese, and porter. The witness had not seen him since, and Mr Cook confirmed this in his statement.

Another witness, Constable John Hewitt from Birmingham was called. He had been ordered to search the prisoner's lodgings at an

---

1. A promissory note of guaranteed payment.

address in Canal Street, where he shared a room with a Mr John Vaughan. Mr Vaughan was present during the investigation, and the constable found a portmanteau with shirts marked with the name "Mister" on them and a razor with a black handle. Mr Vaughan explained that he had loaned the prisoner an 'unset' razor, but the one produced did not match the one found in Whatmore's Yard in Ludlow which was 'set.'

After the constable's statement, Mr Valentine Lee, the defence barrister, who had yet to cross-examine any of the witnesses, was making numerous notes.

The next witness was George Hathaway, ostler[2] at the Angel Inn, Ludlow, who had found a pair of stained, white, unbleached cotton stockings wrapped in an old newspaper in the brewhouse adjoining the inn. He reported that he had given them to Mr Davies, the gaoler, who later gave them to Mr Hodges, the surgeon, but he could not identify the stain.

Mr Valentine Lee stood up and addressed the jury for the first time, reminding them that they must only consider the facts put before them in the court of law and must not be in any doubt of their final verdict against the prisoner. He then sat down and began writing again.

The next witness, Mr George Green, confirmed that he was a servant of Mr Nelson Bagley, a banker of Shrewsbury, and on the night in question, he had slept at the Angel Inn. He recalled how he had seen the prisoner in his night-shirt in a stooping position outside Mr Mackreth's door about ten minutes after the cry of "Fire" was raised.

Another witness was a Mr John Cross, a tin man by trade, who resided in a house opposite the Angel Inn. He explained how he had been alarmed by the cry of "Fire" in the early hours and woke his wife, who always slept soundly. He went out into the street and saw Mr Cooke, the landlord, at the door of the inn looking up and

---

2. A man employed to look after the horses of people staying at an inn.

down the street in a distressed manner. Mr Cooke asked him if he had seen anyone, but the street was deserted. Mr Cross followed Mr Cooke upstairs and noted that there were spots of blood outside room number 17 on the carpet, with more pools of blood continuing around four or five inches apart leading to room 20. The carpet stopped about six inches from the door, and he could see more blood on the floor next to the door. He did not share these observations with anyone at the time because the whole inn was in a panic, but he later told the constable who was taking statements. When he finished, Mr Cross was thanked by the judge and sat down next to his wife who was visibly proud of her husband's star witness performance.

During this initial evidence, Josiah Mister kept his head bowed or stared intensely at the jury box. Those jurors who caught his eye immediately looked away from his black penetrating gaze. William, on the other hand was busy making notes and whispering to Henry or a member of his legal team.

Meanwhile, both William and the accused had caught the attention of two respectably dressed women in the gallery, a Mrs Florence Beaton, and a Mrs Violet Splatt. Both their husbands were in trade and doing very well for themselves in the town of Shrewsbury. Mr Alfred Beaton was the town's biggest ironmonger, supplying most of the surrounding farms and had a reputation for a good a fair service in the community. If there was anything he did not have, he would always source it for a customer, like his father before him, something he was teaching his two young sons who had also joined him in the business. Mr Zachery Splatt was the town's main haberdasher and most of the ladies in the gallery would in fact have been his customers one way or another. "I quite like the look of the one in the dock." Florence whispered to Violet. "Shame on you Florence Beaton," Violet replied, "the man's a criminal."

"I don't care." she replied. Violet hesitated before saying with a cheeky grin, "Come to that, neither do I. I prefer the gentleman with the scar. But if push came to shove, I would not say no to either." They both let out a cackle like a couple of hens and the sound vibrated around the court bringing hundreds of pairs of eyes upon them and the steely gaze of the Judge Sir John Baron Gurney.

"If we have such a disgraceful disruption like that again I will clear the gallery and charge the culprit with "contempt of court!" the judge bellowed in a voice that would put thunder to shame.

Both women wished the ground would swallow them up and did not utter another word. What would their husbands say? They were bound to hear of their disgrace sooner or later as it would be all over Shrewsbury.

The next witness to take the stand was Henry Hodges, a highly respected citizen of Ludlow and surgeon. He was asked to describe the nature of Mr Mackreth's wounds, to which he replied that they were the worst he had ever been asked to attend. "There was a cut from ear to ear through the mouth," he confirmed. This description elicited a further collective gasp from the jury box and the assembled gallery. Mr Hodges went on to say, "There was also a cut to the throat and Mr Mackreth's right hand, and all the wounds were bleeding quite profusely. My main concern was the wound to the face, as the wound to the throat did not appear to be deep enough to damage the windpipe. I feared that too much blood had already been lost and that the patient might not survive. I cleaned his face with spirits, and as I did so, two other medical colleagues arrived to assist and sew up the wounds with silk. Based on the nature of the wounds, I suspect that they were inflicted by a person on the victim's left, as the cuts varied in depth from where the knife or razor first penetrated. There was blood everywhere, but I did notice a trail of blood on the carpet leading from room 17 to room number 20, as well as blood on the walls and carpet down the stairway." The sergeant nodded and thanked Mr Hodges.

The next witness to be called was a Mr R D Crawford, a fellow surgeon from Shrewsbury who had subsequently become a good friend of William's. Mr Crawford confirmed his identity and that he was staying at the Angel Inn in room number 19 on the 20th of

August of last year. It was about four o'clock in the morning when he was awoken by the cry of "Fire" and a general commotion.

"I looked out of my bedroom window and saw in the inn yard below Mr Cooke, the landlord, and a few other people. I immediately dressed and went into the passageway and saw the wounded gentleman who was in the room adjacent to mine. By this time Mr Cooke and another gentleman were also in the room, and there was a great deal of blood everywhere, including on the stairs leading to the landing. I was joined almost immediately by another medical colleague and surgeon, Mr Hodges, who you just interviewed, and we immediately started to render assistance to the gentleman I now know as Mr Mackreth. We were also joined by another colleague, his assistant, and the local Doctor, Edward Lloyd, who had been called by Mr Cooke.

About three-quarters of an hour later, Constable Hammond and I searched the room to see if I could find the instrument which may have inflicted the wounds but only found two white-handled razors in Mr Mackreth's dressing case which had not been used."

"Was there anything else in the room that you noticed?" quizzed the Sergeant.

"I noted the broken windowpanes and the torn curtain and the bloodstains on them. I had blood on my hands, but not enough to cause drops. I did not touch anything apart from the dresser drawer handle and the dressing case to open it. During closer examination, it was discovered that the curtains opposite the foot of the bed that hung across the window were smeared with fresh blood. I had been informed that a bloodstained razor had been found in the yard below the window, so I lifted my hand as if to throw something, and my hand reached about three inches above the stain. I am approximately five feet ten inches tall, while the prisoner is about five feet six and a half inches tall.

Police Officer Hammond and I then proceeded to Mr Whatmore's yard, where the razor had been found. It was directly opposite the prisoner's window. Upon returning to room number 20, we noticed that the water jug was empty, and the slops were still in the chamber utensil. I examined the fluid in the utensil and tasted it." This last statement caused raised murmurs in the gallery and the judge had to call the room to order before the witness continued.

"It was mixed with alum. When asked by the constable to explain what alum is and what it is used for, I replied that I had conducted several experiments with alum, which is commonly used to stop bleeding if one is cut while shaving, and it works very well. It also has another use: it can effectively remove blood stains from clothing." More murmurs and gasps from the jury ensued.

"Later, when the prisoner was taken into custody between the hours of 9 and 10, I noticed that his shirt had several blood marks on the back and two on the sleeve."

"Thank you, Mr Crawford. That will be all."

At this point Mr Valentine Lee was given another opportunity to cross-examine the witness, but he responded by saying, "It is not necessary at this time."

Chapter 3

"I wonder why Mr Lee is declining to ask any questions so far," whispered William to Henry.

"Yes, perhaps the evidence of the witnesses is too damning, and it is unlikely to help the defence." replied Henry. "It is an exceedingly difficult case to defend, but from Mr Lee's deportment and manner, he does not appear to lack confidence. I wonder what cards he has up his sleeve."

William remained deep in thought, debating whether as Henry had intimated, there could be more to Mr Lee's insouciance. Was there a chance that Josiah Mister was not the culprit, and the defence would reveal an alternative explanation? A seed of doubt planted itself in William's mind.

As the arresting officer, Police Constable Hammond was then called to the stand. He confirmed Mr Crawford's findings when he accompanied him to the prisoner's room and what had happened after he and his fellow officers were called to the Angel Inn.

Constable Hammond was then shown Mr Mackreth's nightshirt, which was unfolded with some dramatic fanfare by the sergeant. The garment was torn and completely drenched in blood and its exhibition caused a strong sensation in the court. The prisoner however remained unmoved, just gazing blankly in its general direction. Hammond confirmed it was the one that Mr Mackreth was wearing.

Constable Hammond also confirmed that on inspecting Mr Mackreth's room at a later hour, after the victim had been moved to another room for his comfort and care, he had looked under the bed for clues. He found that there was an outline of a figure in the dust, and a spent Lucifer was also found, along with a piece of sandpaper.

"And what was the length of these measurements?" asked the Sergeant.

"We found that they matched the height of the prisoner."

"Thank you, sir. Can you please tell us more about the whereabouts of the prisoner when you arrived at the Angel?"

"I followed the spots of blood to the prisoner's bedroom door, which was unlocked. I entered and found the prisoner was in bed with the bed clothes pulled over his head, as if he were still asleep." There were murmurings of disbelief and whisperings in the gallery. "No words were exchanged, and I left."

Hammond then added that several other minor witnesses later stated that the prisoner was seen in Mr Mackreth's room, saying he had lost his stockings. Some days later, a pair of white unbleached stained stockings were discovered wrapped in old newspapers in the adjacent stable yard and later handed to Mr Davies, the gaoler. An attempt had been made to clean the stains explained Hammond, so this could have been the reason they could not be positively identified as blood by the surgeon, Mr Hodges.

The sergeant then interjected and stressed to the jury that when the accused was arrested, he had tuppence in his pocket, a small piece of alum wrapped in paper, and some small specks of blood on the back of his shirt.

There was a slight pause in the room before, the judge confirmed whether the sergeant had any further questions. "No further questions at this stage, your honour." The judge turned to Mr Valentine Lee and, as if awakened from a slumber, the defence lawyer suddenly stood bolt upright. Like a lead actor making his debut on a grand stage, he demanded the attention of the whole room. His eyes circled around, and he finally fixed his stare towards the jury and addressed Constable Hammond as he did so.

"Constable Hammond, do you not agree that the use of alum is a common substance used by many gentlemen to stem the blood from razor cuts?"

"Yes, sir," replied Officer Hammond.

"In fact, I use it myself," replied Mr Lee. He paused as if waiting for this piece of information to be fully absorbed by his audience.

"…And the blood spots, could they have not come from any of the numerous people who entered Mr Mackreth's room or climbed the stairs? As has previously been given in evidence, there was blood everywhere and this could surely have been transferred onto clothing or shoes, could it not?"

"Quite possible, sir," replied Officer Hammond, "but in my experience, this results in a footprint or a smudge of blood, not a drop of blood. The blood leading from Mr Mackreth's room on the carpet, leading to the prisoner's room, were definitely drops of blood, sir."

There were further murmurs amongst members of the public gallery. Mr Lee stated that he had no further questions for the moment, and Officer Hammond was excused from the witness box.

Next up on the stand was a Mr Simon Head, an architect from Ludlow who had constructed a model of the rooms at the Angel Inn, who was asked to confirm the accuracy of the room plan and measurements. Mr Head, an elderly and impeccably dressed gentleman who had designed many of the more desirable buildings in Ludlow over his lengthy career, confirmed that he had checked everything himself and could guarantee the authority of the model and measurements. The judge thanked him for his diligence and asked him to stand down.

Mr Valentine Lee then asked the judge if he could examine the model and measurements for a moment, and he did, making notes while peering into the wooden construction quite intently through his half-mooned wire-rimmed spectacles. After a minute or two, he thanked the judge and returned to his seat.

It was now time for the chief witness to take the stand.

Chapter 4

Mr Fairchild requested that his client, Mr William Miller Mackreth, be called to the stand. There was once again chattering in the gallery, to which the clerk of the court appealed for silence. William climbed the steps into the witness box. Given his ordeal, the sergeant thought, like many in the court, he looked remarkably well apart from a faint scar. William was asked to confirm his identity and current residence.

"Mr Mackreth, do you recognise the accused man sitting in the dock?"

"I do. He is the gentleman who entered my bedroom after my wounds had been attended to. I distinctly remember him because he was laughing and assumed a great deal of levity. He kept repeating, *I have lost my stockings! Has anyone seen my stockings?*"

There was a gasp of disbelief from the public gallery, earning them a stern stare but no comment from the clerk, who also appeared surprised. "Did he say anything else?" asked the prosecutor.

"Not that I heard or can remember," said William.

"Thank you, Mr Mackreth. Please be seated."

"May the witness Mr John Cross be called once more?" Mr Cross re-took the stand and was asked by the prosecutor the same question as William, "Do you recognise the prisoner?"

"Yes, sir. It was me who gave the injured gentleman the pen and ink so he could write down the questions being asked of him. I later saw the prisoner leaning on the chest of drawers in the injured gentleman's bedroom. He had no coat or waistcoat on at the time, and when he returned, he had his boots in his hand and was asking about his stockings."

"Anything else?" asked Mr Fairchild

"No, sir," replied Mr Cross.

"Thank you. You may sit down." Mr Cross touched his head and scurried back to sit next to his beaming wife.

Mr Godson for the prosecution stood up and requested that Mr Nathan Cooper be called to the witness stand. A tall man dressed entirely in black entered the box with a slight stoop and identified himself as Mr Cooper, a surgeon from Newport, Gwent.

Mr Godson interjected, "I wish to make a point to the jury before this gentleman continues. So far there has been no positive identification of the weapon in this case. A razor, believed to be the instrument for the attack, has not as yet been established as belonging to the accused. However, this mystery may now be solved. Please tell your story, Mr Cooper."

"I was travelling on the Monday before the Shrewsbury Fair on the road from Bishop's Castle to Shrewsbury, near the village of Longden when I saw a man making a purchase from a pedlar, and when I approached, I could see he was purchasing a razor. He turned to me and asked if I had change of two sixpences for a shilling to enable him to make a bargain. I was able to oblige him, and he made his purchase."

"Mr Cooper, do you recognise the man in the dock?"

"Yes, sir, it was the young man here I saw buying the razor."

"Thank you, Mr Cooper. That is all," Mr Godson said.

As Mr Godson returned to his seat, after a slight pause, his colleague Mr Fairchild stood up and turned to address the Jury. "This, gentleman of the Jury, explains why the razor found at the scene of the crime does not match with the set one from the prisoner's lodgings in Birmingham. He bought another razor! A search has been conducted to try and find the hawker in question to identify the razor as he is known in the villages in the area."

The clerk to the court arose and addressed the judge, confirming that an advertisement had been published in several county newspapers addressed to hawkers, cutlers, and pedlars, asking them if they had recently sold any black-handled razors with the maker's name of Ellis on it and to contact the court immediately. However, as yet, no one had come forward in the months since the advertisement had been placed.

Mr John Humphries was then called at the request of Mr Tom Neale for the prosecution.

"Would you please identify yourself to the court?" Mr Neale asked.

"My name is John Humphries, sir, and I am a servant to Mr Haverham of the Talbot Inn in Church Stretton, which is about 16 miles from Ludlow on the Shrewsbury Road."

"Please tell the court what you saw on the Friday morning, the day after the Shrewsbury Fair."

"I found the man over there," Humphries said, pointing to Mister. "He was lying amongst the hay in the loft of the Talbot Inn. I told him to be off directly before the master found him. He had his boots off and a handkerchief over his head, and he was wearing white cotton stockings on his feet, which were brown at the toes. He said he had walked many miles the day before and was very tired. He asked how far it was to Ludlow and then went off in that direction. He wore a brooch or pin in his stock".[3]

Mister suddenly jumped up and shouted at Mr Humphries, "How did you notice I had a brooch in my stock?"

Unperturbed, Mr Humphries replied, "I could not help but notice. You were stood right in front of me!" There were bursts of laughter from the public gallery.

Judge Baron Gurney brought his gavel down with a loud bang that echoed around the court, causing some of the ladies present to let out a startled cry. "Order! Order!"

Mr Neale thanked Mr Humphries and asked him to be seated. This was the first time he had been asked to be a witness, and it had already made him a celebrity in the local village. This was also only

---

3. A stock is a silk or fine scarf wound around the neck and secured with a pin or brooch.

the second time he had ever been to Shrewsbury in his 29 years of life, and he was enjoying it immensely. The first time was when his late father had brought him to Shrewsbury to buy his very first pair of boots.

The judge thanked him for the information and adjourned the court to tomorrow at half past nine in the morning. All stood and bowed to Sir John, who then left for his chamber.

Chapter 5

On the second day of the trial, the court reconvened, and William and Henry arrived early to confer with their legal representatives. While in deep discussion, an excited court clerk informed them that the hawker had come forward and was on the witness list to be called first. Mr Godson thanked the clerk for the information, enabling them to prepare their questions for a Mr James Bell.

James Bell was a hawker who went by the name of Jimmy and was well-known in the villages where he conducted his trade.

Jimmy had been adopted by a childless couple in his village when his own mother had died giving birth to him. The village blacksmith and his wife, Daniel and Ruth Bell, had given up hope of having children of their own and they welcomed their new adopted son with immense joy. Daniel had hoped to eventually teach him the blacksmith trade but a few years later a tragic accident denied Jimmy that path. His father was shoeing a large working horse when it kicked out, killing him instantly. Ruth and Jimmy's life changed for ever. Everyone in the village showed them great kindness but Ruth had no choice but to sell her husband's business to an outsider from a neighbouring village.

Ruth taught little Jimmy all she knew, and he could write his name and even read a little by the time he was 11. He grew to be a strong lad of a very friendly nature, just like his adopted father. He would do odd jobs for anyone who asked him, and he would help them even if they did not ask him, such was his nature. He earned the odd copper here and there and sometimes even a shilling and everything he earned he gave to his mother. They kept a few chickens and a couple of geese, which they always managed to sell at Christmas time.

They were poor but they about managed on the money Ruth had been given for the forge, the selling of eggs and the money Jimmy earned from his odd jobs. Jimmy had a natural talent for repairing things that nobody wanted and selling them on to make a profit. As he got older, he drew on his talents to become a successful pedlar. He would buy from the bigger merchants in Shrewsbury, everything his mother suggested their fellow villagers would use and often run out of and would be unable to replace until market days. It worked and Jimmy made a decent living, eventually able to buy a small pony a cart allowing him to carry a larger selection of goods. Jimmy had a reputation that if he did not have what a customer wanted, he would get it by the next time he called at their village.

Today, Jimmy found himself in Shrewsbury court being asked to give evidence in one of the most reported cases in the land.

When Jimmy was called to the witness stand, he felt nervous, causing his stomach to ache. Mr Godson asked him if he had been in Bishop's Castle the Monday before the Shrewsbury August fair, to which Jimmy nodded. Mr Godson then asked if he had sold a razor on the day in question, to which Jimmy hesitated briefly before confirming that he had. Mr Godson asked if he were sure, and Jimmy replied that he was, explaining that he only sold a few razors a year as most of his customers had beards, so he could easily remember each sale. After this revelation, there was a brief burst of laughter from the gallery, which was silenced by Sir John's icy stare.

When Mr Godson asked why he bothered carrying razors if he sold so few.

"Just to offer the best service I can to my customers, sir," replied Jimmy proudly.

"Very commendable too, young man," replied Mr Godson with a slight smile. "And would you recognise the razor you sold on that day?"

"Yes, sir. I would recognise the type I sell."

With some fanfare, Mr Godson slowly unwrapped a white cloth in front of him on his desk and held up a black-handled razor. "Is this the razor, Mr Bell?" asked Mr Godson.

"It's the same as the ones I sell, sir."

"Thank you, Mr Bell. No further questions, my Lord," said Mr Godson, looking towards the bench and giving Judge Baron Gurney a slight bow before retaking his seat. After Jimmy's testimony, there were many hushed voices across the courtroom that took a few moments to finally subside.

After a straightening of papers and a clearing of his throat, Mr Valentine Lee rose from his seat and was acknowledged by Sir John, giving him permission to cross-examine the witness. Mr Lee looked at Jimmy for a few seconds, but it seemed like an eternity to the young hawker. He was unsure what to expect next, but he remembered what his mother had told him, "Always respect your elders and betters and don't upset the apple cart, and you won't go far wrong in this life, my lad."

"You are Mr James Bell, are you not?"

"Yes, sir," replied Jimmy with a slight bow. "And you are a pedlar?"

"Yes, sir," replied Jimmy. "Do you recognise this razor?" said Mr Lee, holding up the same razor as Mr Godson had produced. "Is this the razor you allegedly sold to the accused in the village of Bishop's Castle?"

"Yes, sir," said Jimmy.

"Oh, so you can identify this as the exact razor you sold?" exclaimed Mr Lee.

"No, sir," stuttered Jimmy. "I mean, it looks exactly like the one I sold. I only sell one type, sir."

Mr Valentine Lee looked in the direction of the jury and said in a raised voice, "These types of razors are produced in Birmingham in quite large numbers, and no doubt there are gentlemen in this court today who own this same type of razor. I put it to the jury that the razor used in the criminal assault of which the prisoner is accused could have been owned by any number of people and must be dismissed as evidence. No more questions, my Lord." Jimmy was told he could now sit down, and he felt relieved.

For the remainder of the day the focus turned back to the case for the defence. The anticipation and tension in the court was palpable, with a loud hum of voices that even failed to be quashed by the appearance of Sir John as he took his seat. The clerk of the court called for silence in an almost pleading tone, followed by the cold glare of Sir John, which immediately cast a spell of quiet.

Chapter 6

Looking directly at Mr Lee, Sir John requested him to present his case for the defence.

"Thank you, my Lord," said Mr Lee, standing for a moment to turn his head and eyes around the court and finally the jury. Without a doubt, he was an imposing figure, and projected an air of arrogance that suggested he knew it.

"Gentlemen of the jury, you have heard many testimonies and opinions over the last couple of days that attempt to explain what happened on the date of the incident. I am about to demonstrate to the court, that none of the evidence presented thus far conclusively proves the prisoner's guilt. What will be shown is that much of the attestations are based on mere assumptions and are purely circumstantial.

I put the following points to you for your consideration and judgment.

First, there is no evidence that categorically proves, without any doubt, that the razor found in the yard adjacent to the Angel Inn belonged to the prisoner. As one of the witnesses, James Bell has just testified, the type of razor found is extremely common and could have belonged to any of the guests staying at the inn.

As most of us are aware in this court today, this case has drawn worldwide attention, having been covered in all the newspapers both in this country and across the Empire. I put it to you that due to the level of hysteria that surrounds this case, much of the evidence that has been collected against my client is inherently biased, tainted, and therefore inadmissible. Josiah Mister has simply become a victim of a witch-hunt.

One such example of this hysteria lies is a statement found recently in the London press that Josiah Mister had been shaved in his hometown of Birmingham several weeks before his eventual journey to Ludlow, and that a razor fitting the description of the one found in Ludlow went missing from the barber's. This story has since been revealed as completely untrue, demonstrating how society as a whole is determined to see an innocent man hang."

These allegations were beginning to make an impact on the jury with many now looking pensive. Until now, the majority seemed convinced of the prisoner's guilt – a very straightforward case. This was the first time that an element of doubt was beginning to creep into their minds. William glanced across at Henry and pursed his lips.

While the jury and court dwelled on what Mr Lee had just uttered, he then proceeded to pull out a long shirt from a cloth bag.

"Gentlemen of the jury, this is the shirt that the prisoner was alleged to have been wearing at the scene of the crime, which I give up to the jury to examine," passing it to the foreman.

As the shirt was passed from one juror to the next, Mr Lee spoke slowly and carefully, "Now, as you can clearly see, there are several obvious stains on the shirt, but is there any sign of blood? Surely, if this is the shirt that the culprit of this terrible crime was wearing, there would be more blood stains. He pointed at the stains. "Look! They are hardly worth looking at. Also, please observe the position of the stains on the back of the shirt and not the front. Would not anyone inflicting such deep wounds be covered in blood themselves? And, indeed, furthermore, that blood would be on the front of the garment, not the back," he declared.

"Then there is the trail of blood leading to the prisoner's room. After the attack on Mr Mackreth, Mr Cook, the Landlord, and several guests staying at the Angel Inn, all had been in close contact with Mr Mackreth in his room where there was a considerable amount of blood, as confirmed by both the surgeons and doctors. Is it not conceivable that they would have blood upon themselves and while walking up and down the corridor, deposited the blood on the carpet outside the prisoner's room or even transferred blood on to the prisoner as they brushed past him? In the general bedlam and commotion, everyone was walking around freely.

Let us now dismiss another piece of evidence as false. The Lucifer match found under the bed should not be considered as implicating the prisoner in any way. The statement by the young boy who was playing with the wasp nest in Church Stretton and claims he was told by the prisoner that he needed a Lucifer match, which he drew from his waistcoat pocket and then replaced, proves nothing. To suggest it was the same Lucifer that was found under the bed is utter nonsense. Lots of people carry Lucifers for all sorts of reasons, and I even carry some myself," he produced and opened a silver box with a grand sweeping gesture. "Like the razor, the Lucifer is a common everyday object, and there is nothing that absolutely shows that the one found at the scene of the crime belonged to the prisoner."

"I would also like to question the evidence of the blood found on the curtains of the prisoner's room. I put it to you that it is quite possible that this could have been transferred there by several persons, including the maid, Mary Fowkes, who had been in Mr Mackreth's room picking up towels that had been used to stem the flow of blood and were completely saturated. Would she not have blood all over her hands, so when she opened the curtains, the blood would have been deposited there? It is telling that no other blood was found in the prisoner's room, and the blood spots leading from Room number 17 to number 20 could also have been left by several persons, including Mr Crawford, the surgeon. Indeed, a trail of blood was also found leading to his room, number 19. Is it not possible that he could have taken a few extra steps, leaving blood outside number 20, the prisoner's room?

As you can see, all the evidence given thus far is severely impaired, and I will continue to offer you reasons why it should be discounted.

Let me be clear. I do not impeach the testimony of any witness, but I do protest against certain inferences made. For example,

Mr Crawford's assumption surrounding the alum found in the chamber pot in the prisoner's room, which has been claimed to have been used to remove blood from the prisoner's items of clothing. This is pure assumption, as it is just as likely it was used in the process of morning washing after a shave, as it stems the flow of blood from razor nicks and small cuts. As many of the gentlemen here today will attest to, it is customary for gentlemen to carry a small piece of alum in their shaving cases.

Another insinuation from the prosecution relates to Josiah Mister's candle burning out. What does that prove? Who of us has not gone to bed and allowed the candle to burn out?

On the early morning of the attack when the alarm was initially raised, Mr and Mrs Cooke, together with the maid Mary Fowkes and the boot boy were the first persons downstairs. We are not aware of whether doors to the inn were open or closed, apart from the door to the yard. Let me put it to the jury that anyone could have entered and left the building without detection and that Mr Josiah Mister is a victim himself in this case. All the so-called evidence used to charge him with this crime is purely circumstantial. I urge the jury to put aside any stories or prejudices they may have and only consider what is irrefutable. The jury must therefore give the prisoner the benefit of any reasonable doubt which exists in their minds after carefully considering all the facts of the case, which I believe to be unparalleled in the annals of criminal jurisprudence.

Looking at all the circumstances and remembering the excellent maxim of Lord Hale, 'It is better that five guilty persons should escape than one innocent man suffers', I trust the jury will regard the position of the prisoner with all the charity, justice, and providence that our Christian values and the law requires."

Mr Lee turned away from the jury, looked towards the judge, and bowed slowly. "I rest my case, my Lord."

The forceful defence had lasted for an hour and a half – concluding with Mr Valentine Lee telling the jury that law, justice and religion demanded a verdict of not guilty.

There was a lull in proceedings as a hush descended on the courtroom and its members started to digest the words of Mr Lee and their implications. The conclusions of the jury were now being clearly challenged and despite the convincing arguments of the prosecution and the rhetoric of the press, there was now for the first time some uncertainty being cast on whether the prisoner in the dock was innocent of the crimes he was accused.

William whispered into Henry's ear, "I almost began to believe what Mr Lee was saying. Perhaps this fellow is indeed subject to a miscarriage of justice?"

"My dear brother, Mr Lee is certainly a very astute and clever man, but I still feel the jury will listen to reason. It is too fantastical to imagine that anyone, but Mister could have been responsible." William was not as sure as his brother and felt some of the old anxiety return. He reached for his handkerchief to wipe his brow as his legs tightened and pressed together and his mind raced back to the night in Ludlow.

During the whole proceedings, William had noticed that the prisoner had conspicuously avoided his gaze, but it was at this moment that their eyes locked together, just for few seconds. For the first time in Mister's countenance there was glimmer of fear in his eyes as he awaited his fate. The moment soon passed as both men quickly looked away. The two brothers and the rest of the court waited for the prosecution to respond. Perhaps, thought William, Mister was looking for some kind of redemption or mercy for what he had done. Or was it, as Mr Lee suggested, a case of a hunted man, pursued for a crime he did not commit by a misguided and blood-thirsty lynch mob?

Chapter 7

The judge motioned for a small recess in proceedings before the prosecution began their final arguments. The collective jabbering of the crowd made it difficult for William and Henry to converse without raising their voices.

"That was quite an impressive performance from Mr Lee," said William.

"Indeed," responded Henry. "He has done a convincing job of casting some doubt, however small, in the minds of the jurors. But William, I still believe that the prosecution's evidence will result in justice being served."

William was not sure what to believe and was also unsure how he would feel, whatever the verdict.

The clerk of the court rose and requested the prosecution to deliver its final summation.

The sergeant slowly rose to his feet. His imposing six-foot figure towered over the seated jurors as he briefly smiled.

"The offences of which the prisoner has been charged were committed in the early hours of the morning of August 20th last year, at the Angel Inn in the town of Ludlow. On that morning, just after four o'clock, Mr William Miller Mackreth was awoken out of his sleep by a violent attack and found himself to be severely wounded. The overwhelming evidence from this felonious attack clearly points to the prisoner being guilty of this crime."

All the faces of the court turned towards the prisoner. He looked much younger than his 25 years. With a sallow complexion and gaunt appearance, he now looked quite pitiful. His countenance remained calm, with little clue towards his inner emotions. As he felt the eyes of the court upon him, he directed his eyes briefly upwards towards his only supporters, his father and two brothers who were seated in the first row of the public gallery.

"Let me take you back to the events that led up to the vicious attack in Ludlow. From all the evidence collected and statements given, the prisoner at the bar, Josiah Mister was in Shrewsbury on August 12th last year for no apparent lawful reason but to make extensive inquiries about a gentleman by the name of Mr Sidney Ludlow, a wealthy butcher and cattle dealer of Birmingham who was known to carry substantial amounts of cash on him.

His motives were clear from the outset. He meant to relieve Mr Ludlow of his riches by any means he could. He connived to find out what room Mr Ludlow was staying in at the Unicorn Inn, but his plans were thwarted as he was to share a room with a colleague that evening.

After leaving the inn the following morning without paying his bill, Josiah Mister made his way to Ludlow where he knew that *Mr Ludlow* was now heading. Now seemingly penniless, Mister walked the 27 miles, planning to meet Mr Ludlow as he stepped off the Red Rover coach.

He purposely pretended to be an acquaintance of Mr Ludlow so that his respectability would be assured, and he could obtain a bed for the night in the same inn by the name of the Angel. His plans had been scuppered in Shrewsbury, but he was now presented with a second chance. He found out from the maid which room Mr Ludlow typically frequented, number 17 opposite the yard, and he began to hatch his evil plan once more.

However, again fate had intervened, and due to the brisk business of the fair, the landlord at the Angel Inn had already given room 17 to another guest who had arrived a day earlier, a Mr William Miller Mackreth, a businessman from Bristol. As we now know, this was fortunate for Mr Ludlow but not so for Mr Mackreth.

During the evening prior to the attack, Josiah Mister even had the audacity to spend the evening socialising with Mr Ludlow, who had recognised him from the Unicorn Inn, such was the cunning of the prisoner to ingratiate himself with his intended victim.

Josiah Mister retired to bed early that evening, and shortly afterwards, he left his room and entered what he thought was Mr Ludlow's room. He then hid under the bed, which was only nine inches deep from the racking, later leaving a stain on the wooden floor caused by the accused's breath mixed with dust." The Sergeant looked meaningfully towards Mister, who was of a very slight build, insinuating to the court that only a very slim person could be accommodated under the bed.

"Armed with a razor, a piece of sandpaper, and a Lucifer, he quietly waited for his victim. It must have been extremely uncomfortable for him, but he waited and waited until a person who he thought was the person he had followed all the way from Birmingham was shown into the room by the chambermaid, Susan James.

Mister would have heard the person undress, blow out his candle, and climb into bed. In a busy inn like the Angel, there would still have been many comings and goings until the early hours. So, the prisoner needed to wait for the perfect opportunity. With one swift and noiseless cut, he planned for it to be all over for his victim. He would then retrieve the gold, return to his room, act as normal, and leave early the next morning before any suspicions were aroused.

All was silent at last. It had been hours and hours of waiting, but now was the time. He slowly crawled from under the bed with the open razor in his right hand. He could see his victim before him as his eyes adapted to the small amount of light coming from behind the curtains. He reached down and made a grab with his left hand for the chin of his victim but missed and caught the side of his face. His victim awoke as the slash of the razor caught his hand. Panicked, the attacker made a backward movement of the razor, cutting the victim's face from ear to ear. But his victim was still struggling. Another slash caught his throat, and the attacker now began to realise that this was a much stronger and younger man than he thought. Fearful that he might overpower him, Josiah Mister pushed past his victim to flee the scene. Meanwhile, the disoriented William Mackreth attempted to shout for help.

Josiah Mister made his way in the direction of the door, where luckily, the key was still in the lock. He pushed the key in the lock to release the door, rushed down the corridor back to his own room, closing the door behind him. His candle was almost out. There was blood on his stockings and shirt. The razor was still in his hand, so he sought to rid himself of the weapon. He went to the window, pulled back the curtains, opened the window, and threw the razor as far as he could into the Baker's yard next door. Then, with the light still emitted from the stump of his candle, he poured water into the chamber pot, added the alum he had in his possession, and attempted to scrub off the blood from his clothes. He succeeded in cleaning the blood from the front of his shirt but overlooked the ones on the back. His stockings remained badly stained with blood, and he knew he would need to dispose of those somehow."

Sergeant-in-law Fairchild took a breath as he surveyed the court, which was deadly silent. "That, gentlemen of the jury, is what I put to you happened on that dreadful night when this horrendous and despicable crime was carried out, and as the evidence shows beyond any doubt, by the prisoner here who sits before you, Mr Josiah Mister.

The blood trail leading to his room, the blood on his room curtains, the razor found in the yard, the attempt to clean the blood off his shirt with alum, the hidden stained stocking, which he continually claimed to have lost and was later found in the brew house. These are all unmistakable evidence of a cold and premeditated crime, fuelled by pure greed and a callous willingness to meticulously plan and perpetrate a foul and brutal murder. Make no mistake, the intention was to kill, and if it were not for the intervention of God's grace, Mr Mackreth would not be here today.

You see before you a cold-blooded killer who has perpetrated a vicious, debased, and devilish act on an innocent man."

Josiah Mister was now staring directly at Mr Fairchild and defiantly mouthing something under his breath, which no one could hear.

The sergeant-in-law bowed to the judge and said in a loud, distinctive voice, "I rest my case, my Lord."

Sir John Baron Gurney shuffled through the papers in front of him before looking towards the jury and summing up, "You have heard the serious charges made against the prisoner and the evidence presented by both the defence and the prosecution. The difficulty of this case," he told the jury, "is whether the blood found on the prisoner's shirt came from the wounded man when the wounds were being dressed or when they were inflicted. But quite possibly the most critical issue in the case relates to the bloodied razor. The circumstances of the razor being found in the neighbourhood of the inn so soon after where the attack was committed affords the strongest conclusion that it was the weapon by which the wound was inflicted and that it must have been thrown there from the inn. It was found opposite the window of the prisoner's room, so it may have been thrown there from the bedroom window or the window in the passage. The final question is, by whom could the act have been committed, unless by the accused? The prisoner was destitute, he had made enquiries about a person known to carry substantial amounts of money, he pretended to be a passenger on the Red Rover coach and obtained ready access to the inn. He had both the means *and* the motive.

You must now carefully consider what you have heard over the last few days and come to a lawful decision. If you have any reasonable doubt whatsoever, you must only return a verdict of not guilty."

There was a loud murmur within the court, and Sir John retired to his chambers for his customary refreshment.

The jury retired to deliberate and returned after just 35 minutes.

The foreman of the jury stood up and Sir John asked him if they had reached a verdict.

"Yes, my Lord. The verdict is unanimous. We find the defendant.... guilty."

Cheers erupted from the gallery and could be heard outside by the waiting crowds who echoed their sentiments. William looked towards Mister. His pallor had turned to grey, and he slumped back as if hit by a physical blow to his whole being. He covered his face and tried to regain his composure. The clerk asked him why he should not die in accordance with the law. He replied in a subdued and trembling voice, "I am not guilty of it."

The Judge picked up his black cap, placed it on his head and declared to Mister that he should prepare for death by asking for mercy in the next world.

"The sentence of the law is that you be taken hence to the place whence you came and there hanged by the neck until you are dead. May the Lord have mercy on your soul."

The judge announced that the punishment would be carried out in ten days' time on the 3rd of April. Josiah's face was now completely drained of any colour.

William and Henry looked at each other with slight disbelief and shock. They had been told by counsel that the sentence would likely be deportation or hard labour, not death. William and Henry were aware that English justice could be harsh and cruel – only 20 years prior a woman was hanged for stealing a sheep. Thankfully, execution had ceased to be handed down for many crimes that once carried the death sentence.

Betraying his intense mental agony, Mister was led away and had to be helped back to his cell. He would later be transported back to Shrewsbury prison when the crowds had dispersed, although there were some determined to see him taken, however long the wait. When he eventually left the court with his jailers in an enclosed carriage, he was met with cries of "Murderer! Hang him now!" and boos from the stalwarts who had stood in the heavy rain. The constables had to hold them back from the coach when it stopped to allow the huge gates to open.

Chapter 8

William and Henry swiftly left Shrewsbury for Bristol, having no desire to witness the sentence being delivered. Affected by the severity of the verdict and the fact that he was simply grateful to be alive, William had already forgiven his attacker. He planned to write to the judge to ask for leniency and a second chance for the young man.

Meanwhile, in Birmingham, Josiah Mister's well-connected brother John was leading a campaign to the Home Secretary, Sir James Graham, for clemency. The proposed victim, Mr Ludlow, and the foreman of the jury who found Josiah guilty were also among the supporters who had already signed the petition. They planned to travel to Bristol to meet with William and ask him to sign the petition if they could persuade him, then travel to London to present the document themselves before the hanging date arrived.

Upon arriving home in Clifton, William and Henry were initially greeted by hugs and kisses by the family at the Mackreth residence. As Jane was near her lying-in time, she had stayed at their new house in Montague Hill. The welcoming party included all the Mackreths, Jane's siblings, Henry's fiancée Anne and her parents, as well as Jane's father, who now needed assistance with a cane to support him.

According to Jane's sister Mary, everything had gone well with the house alterations while William was away, and Jane hoped that he would approve of them. There was also talk of a grand party planned for the following evening at the Brights' in Redland, but all William wanted to do was to go home to Jane where she was there eagerly waiting for him with Mrs Brooks.

When William finally made his excuses and a cab took him to Montague Hill, he felt the emotion of the last days well up inside. When he saw his beloved Jane again, he gently pulled her to him and kissed her. As he squeezed her, William felt the tensions of the last days release as the loving arms of his darling wife cocooned him like a blanket. The couple were not shy in Mrs Brooks' presence. Jane looked radiant, thought William, and once more he felt so blessed to have such a beautiful wife to share his life with.

William was interested to see the house alterations, but he was also extremely tired and still hungry, even after the tea and cake at his father's house. He asked for a little rest and some refreshments before Jane might show him what she had done to the house. A few hours later, Jane led William into the drawing room, and he was immediately impressed by what she had achieved. It certainly met with his full approval, and he could not help but think he had a very talented and capable wife. They then sat together on the sofa and admired the decorations. Jane was anxious to hear what had happened in Shrewsbury, but she desisted from questions as she could see he could hardly keep his eyes open and soon fell into a gentle doze. Jane watched him as he slept, imagining the toll of the trial after waiting so long for it to be over. With it behind him, she hoped it would be a fresh start for them all.

Jane was happy to sit in the drawing room and continue with some embroidery as she listened to William's gentle snoring. Three hours later, William began to stir and immediately apologised for nodding off. Jane would not hear of it, although she found it hard to contain her excitement about finally showing William around the rest of their newly decorated home. Jane felt both proud and honoured to have been given the responsibility for the interiors. In the 1840s, it was rare for a man to entrust his wife to manage such things, as the man was still seen as the 'Master of the House' and everything was by his approval only. William was a man who did not care too much for convention, and it was a quality that Jane was hugely attracted to.

William thought everything was as practical and comfortable, as a home should be. There was a good water supply and a newly designed water closet with pumped water and a tank. His study was just as he would have designed it himself, William was delighted with the results and told Jane so.

"How did you manage to get Mrs Brooks away from your father?" asked William.

"She insisted," said Jane. "Cassie is there now, and according to Mrs Brooks, she has come on in leaps and bounds and is now quite capable of all the household chores. Dolly Perkins is also doing very well, so father is in safe hands and was quite happy for Mrs Brooks to stay for a while. She has been an absolute treasure, and she and Isabella get on like a house on fire. In fact, they all do, and I could not be happier, especially now that you are home, William, and the baby will soon be here, and Henry will be getting married soon. We all have so much to look forward to."

"Has Dr Barber been keeping an eye on you?" asked William.

"Of course, my darling," said Jane. "I only have to sneeze, and Mrs Brooks or Isabella sends for him!"

"Excellent," said William. "I have just been so worried being so far away from you."

"All the family have been so attentive while you've been away, writing daily and paying visits," said Jane.

The couple slept soundly that night, apart from when Jane felt the baby move a few times. It was as though William had shed a huge burden that he had been carrying, and he was almost overcome with the relief he felt.

The following day, William shared everything that had happened in Shrewsbury, as well as the final verdict. Jane could see that William was quite upset by the capital punishment that Josiah Mister had been given by the judge. Jane felt immensely proud that her husband should show such compassion in spite of the daily reminder in the mirror of what this gentleman had inflicted upon him.

He explained to Jane that he would write to the Judge to request a lesser penalty for this godforsaken man. A day later, he received a letter from John Mister pleading with him to add his name as a Christian gentleman to the petition. William replied immediately and suggested a date to meet in four days hence from the date of his letter, at a convenient place near to the coach arrival point. William suggested the coffee house next to the Bristol Nails[4], which was only a few hundred yards from the mail coach arrival point where there were good lodgings nearby for their overnight stay, before continuing their journey to London with the petition.

---

4. This landmark referred to four large round brass pedestals called the Nails with a raised lip to stop coins falling off. These were situated outside The Corn Exchange, on Corn street. Money was placed on the surface of the nail to signify a deal had been struck, hence the saying "pay on the nail".

Chapter 9

Four days later, William arrived at the coffee house and recognised several familiar faces, who invited him to their table. Arthur Mumford, the head brewer whom William knew from the Georges Brewery, asked what he was doing there at that time of the day. William told them the full story of the events in Shrewsbury, and they all agreed that justice had been done, and he should hang. "Well!" said Arthur. "You're a better man than me sir, but you must do what your conscience dictates."

After thanking them for the coffee, William headed to the coach stop, where he could hear the horn in the distance heralding the coach's imminent arrival. Among the passengers, William spotted Mr Ludlow, followed by the foreman of the jury and an older version of Josiah Mister, but of bigger build. Mr Ludlow waved at William to make sure he had seen them, and they walked towards him. John Mister was the first to reach him and clasped William's outstretched hand with both of his. Mr Ludlow gave William a hearty handshake, and the foreman of the jury introduced himself as Edward Thatcher, a candle-maker by trade in Shrewsbury.

William was pleased to see them and asked them to follow him to the coffee house, which was just around the corner next to the Corn Exchange. As they entered, Arthur and his party looked up and stared at the new companions, but the visitors did not notice they were being watched. As they all sat down, William asked where they were staying for the night. Mr Ludlow replied that they were booked to stay at the Hatchet Inn and were hoping William could point them in the right direction. William knew the inn well and assured them it was not too far away, and a cab would get them there in about ten minutes. He added that it had a reputation for good victuals and cleanliness, so they should be quite comfortable.

"Thank you, my dear sir, for agreeing to see us. It is a most Christian gesture." William could see a slight sign of tears welling up in John Mister's eyes. He continued with a sincere and contrite demeanour, "I wish to express my family's sincere and deepest apology for what my brother did to you. It was complete madness and cannot, in all honesty, be explained. We tried to give him every opportunity to lead a prosperous and Christian life, but much to the family's shame and distress, he decided to take another path."

William listened attentively, showing empathy, and understanding for the family's plight before saying, "It is a very regretful situation for you, and I am deeply sorry that you are having to bear this burden. It is not for you to apologise although the gesture is appreciated. I just hope that your brother can in the future be given another chance to lead a different life. So, with that in mind gentlemen, let us get down to the purpose of your visit."

With that, John Mister produced a document from his luggage, which had been inserted into a leather-bound cover, and he put it down in front of William to read. As he read the pages, it was as he expected, a plea for leniency in the form of hard labour or deportation for life. There were several pages of signatures, and John Mister produced a travelling pen and ink box for William's signature. The number of names was certainly impressive, but the weight of adding the victim's signature to the list would hopefully, believed John Mister, spare his brother's life.

John Mister looked up at William and waited. There was no hesitation on William's part as he put pen to paper. "There you are, gentlemen, and I wish you godspeed and every success in your mission." John Mister could tell that William truly meant it. They all shook hands, and William advised them that any cab would take them to the Hatchet Inn.

"Have a safe journey tomorrow," said William as he bid them farewell. He never saw any of the gentlemen again.

When William arrived home, Jane had already retired for the evening, so he retreated to his study and poured himself a drink, reflecting on the events of the past week. The trial was over and he could return to his old life, even though he knew that things had changed, and so had he. He truly hoped that Josiah Mister could be given a second chance, just as he himself had been given, after narrowly escaping death.

Life must go on, he told himself, and there was so much to look forward to – his first child and his brother Henry's wedding. As he settled into bed next to Jane, he remembered that Henry was calling by tomorrow and there was much to discuss. Moments before falling into a deep sleep, he thought about the future and all the exciting possibilities it held.

Chapter 10

At the Bright household, Mrs Brooks had returned and updated everyone with the news from the Mackreth household. Cassie had done a grand job while Mrs Brooks was away, and she was proud of the young girl's progress. Unfortunately, Cassie would be leaving soon to get married and only had two more weeks to go in the Bright household. Dolly Perkins would be her replacement, and Mrs Brooks was already thinking about how she could train her.

Cassie and Isaac's wedding was fast approaching, and everyone was excited about it. They would be getting married at St Philip and St Jacob Church, and Bridget from Mr William Snr Mackreth's household would be coming in to look after Mr Bright for the few hours they would be away. The house was full now, with Joseph living at home again, and Mary, who had finished her studies, was deciding what to do next. Aunt Clarissa had suggested that she teach at her school, but Mary needed more time to think.

As the kitchen bustled with activity, Mrs Brooks could not help but wonder what Cassie's married name would be. She asked Cassie if it were a secret or if she would share it with them. Cassie stopped rolling the pastry and looked up, explaining that she originally thought it would be Hanover because of the firm's name, but it was Kemp, and she would be Mrs Kemp. Mrs Brooks was relieved they got that straight. Not the brightest spark in the fire but Cassie was a good, honest girl who had become quite a good cook. She would miss her. Mrs Brooks suggested they now needed to focus on the present, though, as Cassie was not Mrs Isaac Kemp quite yet.

Some weeks later William eventually received the news that a reprieve had not been granted by the home secretary and the execution had gone ahead. He was much grieved and prayed for mercy on Josiah Mister's soul. Despite everything that had happened, he had not wished for this. However, the inner turmoil that the news naturally triggered was soon dispelled by events happening in William's own life. He was jolted back to reality when Jane showed signs of going into early labour. Dr Barber had to be called, but to everyone's relief, it was a false alarm. According to the doctor, she had still a month to go to full term.

As Cassie's time to leave the Bright Household arrived, there was an air of sadness, but everyone tried to put on a happy face.

"There you are, Miss Cassie." It was the master's voice. Cassie quickly spun round from the kitchen sink, swiftly wiped her hands, and curtseyed. The master rarely, if ever, came into the servants' areas. "This is a small gift and a thank you from the family to enable you to buy something for your new home," he said, and handed Cassie a small leather purse.

"Thank you for your great kindness, sir," said Cassie, blushing so much she thought she would burst.

"We all wish you every happiness for the future." Being a man of few words, Mr Bright then left the kitchen and headed for his study. He was fond of Cassie. She was always a cheerful little soul about the house, and he never saw her looking glum. He would be sorry to see her go, and hopefully he thought, the new girl would do as well under Mrs Brooks' guidance.

As soon as the Master had left, Mrs Brooks and Dolly were around Cassie like flies around a jam pot, curious as to how much was in the purse. Cassie carefully opened the drawstring, and three sovereigns bounced onto the table. They all gave a little gasp, and Cassie stood open-mouthed. She had never seen so much money and wanted to say something, but the words would not leave her lips. Then they all started to shed a tear, and Mrs Brooks bent over and gave Cassie a kiss on the forehead, and as she did so, said the magic words, "There, there, I will get us all a glass of sherry. I am sure the master will not mind on this occasion. Just make sure you put that money in a safe place, you lucky girl."

Later that morning, there was another surprise for young Cassie. A messenger arrived at the door and handed over a small parcel to Mrs Brooks, addressed to Cassie from Jane and William Mackreth. Mrs Brooks returned to the kitchen and handed the parcel to Cassie, who, thanks to Mrs Brooks, could read a few words so knew who it was from. Everyone crowded around while she opened the parcel, which contained a little box and a handwritten note that Cassie read very slowly and then handed to Mrs Brooks. Dolly Perkins could not read either, but Mrs Brooks was working on it, so she read it to them both.

Dear Cassie, just to congratulate you on your forthcoming marriage, and I hope you will be as happy as William and me. Please accept this little memento of your stay at the Bright Household and for helping to look after my dear father. Yours sincerely, William and Jane Mackreth.

Cassie smiled at Mrs Brooks and carefully opened the little black velvet-lined box, revealing a necklace with a bright red flower pendant made of two coloured garnets and real silver, according to Mrs Brooks. "Oh! It's lovely," Cassie exclaimed. "I've never had anything like it before, and I shall only wear it on special occasions. I cannot wait to show my ma. Miss Jane is so kind," she added, tears welling up in her eyes again.

"Don't start that again," Mrs Brooks said with a chuckle. "You'll get us all going, and I have to start thinking about lunch. Your young man will be here soon to pick you up. Are you sure you have packed all your belongings?"

"Yes, I have. Thank you," Cassie replied, dabbing her eye with a handkerchief.

"Let me have a closer look at that pendant, please, Cassie. I recognise that little flower," Mrs Brooks said. "A pound to a penny that's a Bristol Red[5]," she declared as she examined it more carefully. "I've seen them growing in the flower beds up in Clifton village, and if you look at the box, it was made at a jewellery shop in Park Street. Yes, that's what it is, a Bristol Red."

At 12 noon, Isaac arrived on the dot to collect Cassie and transport her to her parents' house. "Cassie," Mrs Brooks said. "There are some of your clothes in the laundry. Run along and fetch them while I answer the door."

Cassie rushed off, raising her hand to her mouth. As soon as he saw Mrs Brooks, Isaac removed his cap. "Hello, Mrs Brooks. I have come to collect my Cassie," he said, entering the hallway.

"Now, young man," Mrs Brooks said, getting straight to the point. "I've grown very fond of Cassie over the last three years, and I want you to make sure you treat her right, or believe me, you will have me to deal with."

"Oh, I will, missus," Isaac replied, forgetting for a second to whom he was talking. "I mean, Mrs Brooks. My da and I will treat her like a princess, honest. I love her very much."

"Enough said then," Mrs Brooks replied, as Cassie appeared in the hallway, clutching her carpet bag with all her possessions, shadowed by Dolly.

Cassie grabbed Isaac by the arm and told him how kind everyone had been and what wonderful presents she had been given. Cassie turned and ran towards Mrs Brooks and gave her a big kiss on the cheek, doing the same to Dolly, who had become a good friend over the last weeks. "Off you go now, and we'll see you tomorrow at the church. God bless you both," exclaimed Mrs Brooks.

---

5. The Bristol Red is a pretty, vibrant red flower reputed to have been brought into the country by the templars. The bright red colour reminded people of the famous Bristol bright red cloth that was produced at the time. Its Latin name is *lychnis chalcedonica* and is also known as the nonesuch flower.

They watched from the door as the cab disappeared down the hill out of sight. "Right," announced Mrs Brooks. "The family will be wanting their lunch soon, and afterwards, we must take up the carpets and put them in the hallway, ready for collection tomorrow by the cleaners. I think it's a bit early in the year, but the master suggested they need a clean."

Chapter 11

The following morning, the carpet cleaners arrived early to collect the carpets, which Mrs Brooks and Dolly had rolled and tied up. "Be careful with those carpets, my lad," Mrs Brooks warned the elder of the two.

"We will, missus," said the young man, doffing his cap.

"And when can we expect them back?" asked Mrs Brooks with a look that said, "Don't trifle with me."

"Friday, missus, without fail," said the one in charge. "Make sure you do," said Mrs Brooks, watching them load the carpets carefully onto their cart and cover them over.

She knew that after cleaning the carpets, they would be dried outside on large lines or spread on the grass at Brandon Hill, with someone to watch over them to prevent theft.

Though it was only mid-spring, the weather had been improving, and they were having some lovely sunny days. Hopefully, tomorrow would be one of them for Cassie's sake.

The following morning, after breakfast, Bridget arrived from the Mackreth household to keep an eye on Mr Bright. Mrs Brooks explained that he was not too steady on his feet these days and showed Bridget where everything was in the kitchen and pantry. Then after introducing Bridget to her Master, she suggested they have a cup of tea.

"We'll have to change into our Sunday best soon and be on our way," Mrs Brooks explained. "We must be at the 'Pip and Jay'[6] by 12 noon and walk to Blackboy Hill first to get a cab. We should

---

6. A nickname for St. Phillip and St. Jacob church in Bristol.

have asked Cassie's young man to arrange it for us. It would have saved us a walk!"

A few hours later Mrs Brooks and Dolly arrived just in time at the church and noticed quite a crowd of friends and family gathered. Isaac and his father were already inside, along with what seemed to be most of the cab drivers and owners of Bristol. As everyone was seated, the organ started to play, and everyone turned around to see Cassie and her bridesmaids coming up the aisle. Mrs Brooks thought how pretty she looked in her dress, carrying a little bouquet of spring flowers, together with the three bridesmaids who looked very much alike, sisters or close cousins she surmised.

After the service, the congregation made their way back to Cassie's parents' little house in St Philips for a meal. Cassie kindly introduced Mrs Brooks and Dolly to everyone, too many names for them to remember, and invited them to help themselves to some food and refreshments. There were pies, pigs' trotters, chitterlings, tripe, brawn, pork, and plenty of boiled vegetables for all, washed down with beer served from large hogshead barrels set up on trestle tables.

In the centre of the table sat a beautifully decorated cake, surrounded by smaller cakes and jellies. Tables were set up both inside the house and in the back yard to accommodate everyone. The best man was playing an accordion, accompanied by Cassie's Uncle Reg playing the spoons, while one of Cassie's cousins entertained the children and adults with clever card tricks.

Mrs Brooks thought what a jolly time everyone was having, as she and Dolly helped themselves to some pie, vegetables, and small tankards of cider. Unfortunately, they could not stay for the cutting of the cake, but Cassie promised to send some to the house while it was still fresh. They said their farewells to everyone and wished the bride and groom every happiness for the future. Cassie and Isaac had extended an invitation for them to visit anytime on their time off, and both Mrs Brooks and Dolly intended to take them up on it.

Chapter 12

One month later, at the Mackreth household in Kingsdown, everyone was busy preparing for the arrival of William and Jane's baby. William was a bundle of nerves and could not get home quick enough every evening to check on Jane's health. His travels had been suspended for the time being, and Christopher George completely sympathised with William's anxiety, particularly as it was their first child. Christopher had become a father six times and had become an old hand, but he could still remember the worry and apprehension of every birth. William was drinking his 'Long John' single malt a bit more than usual, as he felt it helped to calm him. He wondered to himself if he would have coped differently if he had never made that trip to Ludlow.

What also helped to distract him was planning his garden projects and recalling all the tips he had picked up from Jed. The Mackreth house had a large, terraced garden, and William had already decided to plant fruit trees near the bottom wall and a fig tree in the sunniest spot, as he had noticed they seemed to do quite well and bore fruit in the nearby gardens. Knowing he would not have the time to do it all himself, William had decided to employ someone to instigate his plans under his guidance when he could spare the time. Vegetables would be the mainstay, and he wanted to ask Isabella's opinion on what might be useful for the kitchen.

That evening, Henry called in to see them on his way home and give them an update on his wedding plans. He was his usual cheerful self and full of enthusiasm, which was always infectious to anyone in his company. The date had been set, and preparations were in full steam ahead. Henry announced that Anne would love Jane to be the matron of honour if she thought she would be up to it, as it would be in a couple of months' time. Jane did not have to think twice. She loved Henry and had become very fond of Anne, who she now looked upon as another sister.

"Of course, I will be delighted," said Jane. "I shall hopefully be back to normal by then. Please tell Anne I would consider it an honour."

William was to be best man, but that had already been agreed between the pair many weeks ago.

"That's settled then," said Henry. "Anne will be thrilled. Now, you must excuse me. I must now be on my way, or Bridget will have my guts for garters if I am late for dinner again."

He gave Jane a gentle kiss on the cheek, shook William's hand, and strode briskly to the waiting cab outside.

There was a knock on the sitting room door and Ellen Drewett entered, curtseying as she announced that Isabella had prepared dinner. Ellen helped Jane to her feet, holding her arm and assisting her to the dining room. Ellen had fitted in very well, and Jane had become very reliant on her as a personal maid. Forever diligent, Ellen had asked Dr Barber many questions when he came to check on Jane, so she knew what action she should take if Jane went into unexpected labour. She came from a large family and knew the joys but also the dangers and sadness that births could bring, witnessing how her mother had lost two children during childbirth. Little did she know that her knowledge would be required sooner than expected.

That night Jane had experienced a restless sleep that had also disturbed William a couple of times. By six o'clock the following morning Jane was wide awake when she felt a sudden pain that forced a cry of distress followed by "William!" Shaking him awake she gasped, "I think the baby is coming." William leapt out of bed and round to Jane's side, reaching for her hand and forearm.

"Are you sure?" said William in a panicked voice.

"Yes, I'm sure," replied Jane, slightly breathless. "Please call Isabella and Ellen and send Pamela to fetch Dr Barber."

Putting on his dressing gown, William headed out the door in the direction of the staff bedrooms. Halfway up the stairs he met Isabella already on her way down, having heard Jane's cry. Ellen was close behind, having first knocked on Pamela's attic bedroom door, telling her to get dressed.

William followed behind, feeling a little out of his depth amidst three very organised females. He was about to enter their bedroom when Isabella turned around and gently ushered him back. "This is no place for you, sir. We know what to do, and Pamela will bring Dr Barber."

William was distressed by Jane's cries of pain but did as he was told and withdrew to the sitting room. He then changed his mind and headed to his study, poured himself a drink and began to pace up and down.

Meanwhile, Ellen was stoking up the stove for hot water and getting clean linen and towels before changing places with Isabella, who was comforting Jane as best she could.

Pamela was out the door and running as fast as her little legs could carry her. She was in Coldharbour Road in no time, pressing hard and repeatedly on Dr Barber's doorbell. A sleepy-eyed housekeeper answered the door. "It's my mistress," spat out Pamela, wheezing and catching her breath after running all the way. "She is having the babe!"

"Just a minute, I will alert the doctor. What did you say was the name of your mistress?"

"Mrs William Mackreth," said Pamela, now able to breathe normally again.

It seemed like forever before Dr Barber came to the door and asked Pamela with a very quizzical expression, "Are you sure your mistress is having her baby? I would have said she would have at least a few weeks to go."

"Oh, yes," said Pamela, nodding furiously. "She is having it."

"I will get the pony and trap out then, young lady."

The front door of the house was ajar as William waited expectantly in the hallway. William shook Dr Barber's hand and was immediately taken up to the bedroom by Isabella. Ellen had momentarily left Jane's side to collect hot water and extra linen.

As Ellen returned, the baby was well on its way, and Dr Barber gave Jane a dose of laudanum to ease her pain. "Just a few more pushes, Jane," he said. After just a few more contractions, the baby heralded its arrival with a hearty cry. After cutting the cord, the doctor announced, "Congratulations, Mrs Mackreth. You have a healthy baby boy. I will pass on the good news to your husband on my way out." As he left, Ellen wrapped the baby in a blanket and passed the infant to a very weary but delighted Jane.

William, now desperate to see or hear how Jane was, was waiting in the hallway having heard the baby's first cry. "Is my wife alright?" said William, looking at the doctor in sheer panic. Dr Barber smiled and said calmly, "Your wife and your new son are doing very well."

"Oh, thank you, doctor! Thank you!" exclaimed William with huge relief.

"I have given your wife something to help her rest for a while, but you can certainly go and see them within the next half an hour, I would say. A very good morning' to you, sir." And Dr Barber was then on his way back to his warm bed, thinking of the bill he would be sending to William for such an early morning call on his services.

William waited as he was directed, and Isabella and Ellen soon came downstairs, all smiles. "Congratulations, sir," they both chorused, and William, in return, thanked them for all their help and rushed upstairs two steps at a time. "Jane, Jane!" he whispered. She was barely awake as William kissed her and thanked her for their wonderful son. William looked down at his newborn son in his crib. He was all pink and wrinkly with a shock of black hair and fast asleep. William was fit to burst with pride and would start writing letters to all the family, informing them of the happy event straight after breakfast.

Over the next week, the house was packed with visitors coming and going to see the baby and leave presents. Great-Aunt Charlotte arrived in their grand coach and presented them with a silver rattle for the baby's entertainment and a beautifully handmade lace christening gown to use when the time came. Aunt Charlotte also insisted, and no one dared refuse her, that a party be held at their house after the baptism. After much discussion, William and Jane had decided to call the baby, William Henry Mackreth, firstly to honour William's father, as was the family tradition, and secondly to honour his dear brother, who was over the moon when he heard the news. As sometimes happens, in the years to come the young boy asked to be called Henry and became known as Little Henry or Master Henry much to his uncle's delight.

The birth of baby Henry was not only a new chapter in William and Jane's life as parents, but for William it also felt as if the indomitable dark cloud that had dogged him since the trip to Ludlow was beginning to fully dissipate. He began to feel the old confidence and hope that he remembered feeling when he fell in love with his darling Jane on that cool October night in Clifton.

However, immense joy and happiness can often be marred by tragedy, and this was the case for Jane and William. Within months of their son's birth both Jane and William's fathers who had neither been in the best of health, died unexpectedly and in abrupt succession. After both their funerals and a respectable period of mourning, the respective wills were read and decisions made, before both the Mackreths and the Brights settled back once more into the daily routine of their lives.

Jane's younger brother and sister stayed in the Redland house, and Jane had agreed to forgo her inheritance from the house until it was ever sold. Joseph had now qualified as an accountant in the firm he worked for and could afford to keep Mrs Brooks and Dolly Perkins on, much to their relief. Mrs Brooks had been left a handsome sum in John Bright's will in gratitude for all her years of service, but she had no desire to retire. She would look after Master

Joseph as she had his father, his late wife Eleanor, and all the other members of the family since they were children.

Henry, as the second eldest and soon to be married, would take over the Clifton house, and young George and Mary would continue to live in the family home. Anne would join him as soon as they were married, and all the same staff would remain. The Mackreth family business had provided a good income, and all the Mackreth children had been bequeathed handsome sums of money, including the younger members who would inherit when they came of age.

Over the last few years, Henry and George had been running the family business since their father became more infirm, taking on more and more responsibility as time went by. George's interests lay elsewhere, towards the shipping industry, and he and Henry had discussed selling the business if the right offer came along. Henry had no objections, as he and William had also been talking about the exciting potential of investing in the emerging railways, which were sure to take off.

Meanwhile, baby Henry was growing bigger by the day, and Jane was back to her normal self, helping to run the household at Kingsdown, although it really ran like clockwork under the able supervision of Isabella.

Henry and Anne's wedding was also fast approaching, and Anne visited Kingsdown frequently to keep Jane updated on the preparations. During her latest visit, they arranged for Jane and the bridesmaids to meet with the dressmaker and have a final fitting at the vicarage. Anne also shared with Jane Henry's excitement at becoming an uncle and having the baby named after him. "He talks about it all the time and cannot wait for the christening when he will become a godfather," said Anne. The two women settled on a date for the fitting and then enjoyed some tea together.

William arrived home later than usual that evening, and Isabella was fretting in the kitchen that dinner might be spoiled. She was relieved when Pamela returned and confirmed it was William at the door. "I'm sorry, my darling, I'm a bit late," said William to Jane as he kissed her. "I called in to see the Reverend Fouracres to confirm that William Henry will now be christened at St Mary's. He was a bit disappointed but took it in good heart after I explained why. Thinking about it, do you think we should have it before or after Henry and Anne's wedding?"

"Well," said Jane, "I saw Anne today to plan about the dresses, and she was telling me how excited Henry was about his namesake. I think it might be better to have it after the wedding. Too much excitement might not be good for him. Let all the attention rest on Henry and Anne's wedding." They were still laughing when Isabella knocked on the door to announce that dinner was served.

Chapter 13

It was now late summer at Kingsdown House, and the day of Henry and Anne's wedding had arrived. A cab was arranged early to take Jane to the vicarage to join Anne, and Henry planned to pick up his best man later in the morning. Another cab took Ellen Drewett and baby Henry to the vicarage as well, so that Henry could be fed. They had considered hiring a wet nurse, but Jane did not like the idea. Ellen was more than happy to help her mistress, as she treasured the time she spent with the baby. As Ellen departed, Henry arrived, greeted by Isabella, who secretly thought how handsome he looked in his dark grey tailcoat with a velvet collar, light grey trousers, silver-grey cravat, and stovepipe hat, which he had removed upon entering the house. Isabella blushed as she diverted her gaze away from the young gentleman and guided him into the study, where William was waiting.

Dressed identically to his brother, William had ready a couple of glasses, containing a good shot of his favourite whisky.

"Here you are, dear brother. This will calm you down. It certainly works for me."

With a toast of "Slainte Mhath!"[7], something their late father always insisted on when they raised a glass to remember their Scottish roots. The whiskies were downed in one. Henry gave a splutter and coughed, cured by a slap on his back by William, and they were off, arriving at St Paul's with minutes to spare. All the carriages and cabs were lined up with their cabbies and private coachmen with their respective vehicles. William spotted young

---

7. In Scottish Gaelic translates as 'good health'.

Isaac and gave him a friendly wave. Quite a crowd of passersby had collected to watch the event out of curiosity, and William was recognised by many of the well-wishers.

The Reverend Fouracres stood by the main entrance, pacing up and down. After all, it was his daughter who would be getting married today, and he was relieved to see Henry and the best man arrive. As he shook hands with each of them, he urged, "Go in quickly, gentlemen, please. The bride will be here any second." The words had hardly left his lips when two ribboned open carriages appeared into Portland Square and pulled up outside the church. The first carried Anne and her matron of honour, Jane, and the second held all the bridesmaids. The crowd pushed forward for a closer look and uttered words of approval to each other. The Reverend Fouracres thought how beautiful his daughter looked, as did the matron of honour and the excited, noisy, but angelic, bridesmaids. Jane gently hushed the bridesmaids, and Reverend Fouracres kissed his daughter on the cheek, telling her how proud he and her mother were of her.

As they entered the church, all the congregation turned to see the procession as the music started. Ladies reached for their handkerchiefs, and Lillian Fouracres felt quite overcome at the sight of her daughter, her only child, and had to be supported by her sister to help regain her composure. Standing at the altar, Henry was visibly shaking as his bride finally reached his side and he turned to gaze at her. The service was being conducted by a family friend of the Fouracres, a Reverend Paul Townsend, and so Reverend James Fouracres with great emotion gave his daughter away before joining his wife and tightly holding her hand.

The service went smoothly and rose petals soon cascaded down as the happy couple made their way to the waiting carriage, followed by cheers from the crowd of onlookers. They were soon on their way back to the vicarage, followed by all the other carriages and cabs. Realising that a clergyman's stipend was not a fortune, Great-Aunt Charlotte had generously insisted to Reverend Fouracres that she help with the celebration. She had kindly sent over some of her cooking staff with pre-prepared foods, the best wines, and vintage champagne. Henry also offered some financial help, much to the Reverend Fouracres' protestations, but the offer was accepted gracefully in the end. Everyone had a wonderful time at the reception, and when baby Henry arrived with Ellen Drewett, Jane was able to feed him before he was presented to all the relatives for their fuss and approval.

Henry and Anne would be spending their honeymoon at the Mackreth House, while Mary would take a small holiday with relatives in Cirencester and Joseph would be working but staying with friends in nearby Brislington Village for a week or so before returning home. It meant the couple would have the house to themselves, apart from Bridget and Florence, and they would endeavour to be seen and not heard.

Chapter 14

After Henry and Anne's wedding, followed by young Henry's christening, life and business returned to normal for all the Mackreths. Surprisingly, many thought, William visited Ludlow again many times on business and always stayed at the Angel, now run successfully by Elizabeth Cooke who always made him especially welcome. Her husband Edward Cooke had died not long after he had discharged himself from the lunatic asylum, where some say he had placed himself after a rumour that Josiah Mister had an accomplice. The finger had been pointed at him, and many became more suspicious when Cooke discharged himself quite conveniently, some say, after the court case was over.

The escapades of Nellie Winters, the maid at the Angel Inn who had shown Josiah Mister to his room that fateful night, finally caught up with her and she became pregnant by one of the guests staying at the Angel who had fallen for her charms, at a price of course. Faced with destitution, poor Nellie feared she would lose her job, become penniless and she and her mother would be thrown out of their little cottage and be sent to the poor house. She decided to keep her secret for as long as possible so she could earn as much money as possible for when the baby arrived. How could she have become so careless…. She did, however, have a vague idea who the father was.

It had been a quiet time at the inn, when one stout middle-aged gentleman of means stayed there on his way from Herefordshire to Birmingham. He had taken a great fancy to Nellie, and she had immediately surrendered herself to him and was well paid with a golden sovereign. And so, she thought, that was that. However, the stars must have been shining on Nellie, for a couple of months later the gentleman stopped at the inn again, arriving in his own carriage with two drivers and a postillion. He sought Nellie out and made it quite clear he would like her favours again. That evening when the house had closed for the night Nellie went to the gentleman's room, where he was waiting with eager anticipation. Within minutes their pleasures were all over and Nellie burst into tears. The gentleman tried to comfort her and asked her what the matter was.

Nellie told her story and her plight and that he was to blame, imagining she might get a little extra money if he felt sorry for her.

"I 'ave a baby in the oven sir, and you be the one that put it there." she spluttered between sobs and tears. He listened patiently and after a few moments' contemplation, he then grabbed her by the waist, kissing her passionately.

"Marry me, Nellie," he said.

"What?" exclaimed Nellie in disbelief.

"Marry me," he repeated. Nellie thought she would faint. "I have a large estate in Herefordshire and live with my elderly father who has given up on my philandering ways. I need a wife and heir to share it with and I promise to make you happy."

"Yes, I will," said Nellie, not really comprehending what she had just uttered.

"I am the happiest man alive," he whispered in her ear as he pulled her to him.

Mrs Cooke could not believe her ears when Nellie told her and the other chambermaids the following morning. Arrangements were made that he would pick Nellie and her mother up in his carriage in four days' time, on his return from Birmingham, and he gave Nellie ten sovereigns to settle her affairs. Nellie left her job for the last time and headed home to tell her mother the remarkable story. Nellie then took her mother to the best milliners in town, and both were adorned in clothes they never ever thought they could buy. They also bought a large trunk for their meagre belongings and gave the rest away to family and friends. Nellie's new beau was a gentleman named Edward Somerset and four days later he returned for Nellie and her mother. The mother and daughter were waiting, surrounded, so it seemed, by most of the town. Nellie looked quite voluptuous, and Edward grinned widely, like a cat who got the cream, as he alighted from his carriage.

Looking back and closing the door of their little rented cottage Nellie and her mother made their way down the path where they were both helped into the carriage by the postillion and Edward. With all the luggage loaded, they were away to Herefordshire and a new life.

No one at the Angel Inn ever saw Nellie again, but rumours reached them a year later that she had given birth to a baby boy, and she was living the life of a country lady, and everyone was very happy, including Edward's father who had become very fond of Nellie's mother who he found most entertaining.

Life continued for the Mackreth and Bright Households as one might expect. Eventually all the siblings married and raised their own families and Mrs Brooks heard the good news that young Cassie had given birth to a baby boy called David and she proudly accepted the invitation of becoming the baby's godmother. Mrs Brooks stayed in the Bright household happily looking after Master Joseph, who married a friend of his sister Mary, who had finally decided to become a teacher at her aunt's school in Westbury-on-Trym. Having always refused to retire, Grace Brooks died peacefully in her bed at the age of 72.

William and Jane went on to have eight children altogether. Sadly, two of the Mackreth's children died young, including their beloved first-born, Henry, who succumbed to cholera[8] at 23, and a

---

8. In 1830, Bristol was described as a vast and dirty city with a population of 104,408 and was considered the third unhealthiest city in England. It was plagued by a poor water supply, overflowing privies, open drains, and contaminated rivers of both the Avon and Frome, making it a breeding ground for diseases like cholera. The graveyards were constantly overflowing and the stench was unbearable.

younger sister, Catherine, who died at the age of two. William and Jane were married for 20 years, a union that was cut short by the death of William from cancer, aged 50, in 1860. Jane died 19 years later from a stroke at the age of 63. William and Jane were buried together with their children Henry and Catherine at Arnos Vale Cemetery, Bristol, close to the Anglican Chapel.

William would never of course be the same person that he was before taking that fateful trip to Ludlow. He was more watchful and more aware of every step he took in life. He was more mindful of those who were less fortunate than himself, he tried to see things from another's perspective and in business he always listened to others rather than spoke first. The brush with death at such an early age had taught William the value of each day, something one might only realise when one's days were short.

He still thought often of poor Josiah Mister and wished for both their sakes that they had never met and that as Josiah's brother had often hoped, he had taken a different path. Several months after the trial William gradually stopped taking the potion as suggested

---

Springs and wells were highly polluted and no one escaped the effects of cholera, not even the wealthy areas of Clifton and Redland.

At the time no one knew how cholera was spread. Some suggested it was due to miasma, drunkenness, poor ventilation, or rotten meat. It was not until later that contaminated water was identified as the cause.

A Bristol General Cemetery Co was formed consisting of shareholders and Arnos Vale Cemetery was born, hopefully to make a profit and solve the Churchyard scandal. It became a desirable place to be buried by the wealthy citizens of Bristol but paupers were also buried alongside the perimeter walls and eventually cremation became popular and the device is still available to see at the Cemetery's Museum today. Greenbank became the next big Cemetery in the area, followed by Canford.

Despite numerous attempts at cures including electric shock treatment, vapour baths, mercury application, enemas of brandy and turpentine, and leeches, the blight of cholera continued to ravage the city. The burning of tar barrels and juniper berries, whitewashing houses, and increased ventilation were also tried. It was not until later that the City implemented clean water systems and efficient sewage disposal, leading to the eventual subsiding of cases of the disease.

by Dr Barber and he was grateful for such a crutch when he had needed it most.

On his demise, William left most of his wealth to his darling Jane and an annual stipend to his sister Mary who by then was a widow and living in London. Monies were also left to his Church and several charities. The mysterious Ludlow Chest[9], and its contents were left to his son, Edward Bright Mackreth, and has never been found. In Ludlow's history there is a missing Ludlow Chest but that is another story.

---

9. It was the mention of this 'Ludlow Chest ' in William's will that led to his Great, Great, Great Grandson's journey to Ludlow to uncover the mystery, that resulted in the writing of this book.

Epilogue

The Weighing Up

In the spring of 1841, a scaffold was being built above the porter's lodge in Shrewsbury, and the town was abuzz with excitement. Tradesmen were taking in extra supplies in anticipation of the expected surge in business, already convinced of a hanging and hoping that a petition to save the convicted man would fail. After all, business was business.

On the Friday morning of April the 2nd, Josiah Mister's cell door was opened by his gaoler and Mr David Dawson, the governor, who was accompanied by an older man of slight build and a mild expression. Though not introduced, the older man shook Josiah's hand and asked how he was keeping.

"Quite well, considering the burden I have to bear," replied Josiah.

"Quite so," muttered the man to the governor as they left the cell.

Outside and out of earshot, the man informed the governor that he had gauged the man's weight and knew exactly what rope to use. The governor nodded and retired to his office for a much-needed drink. He had never enjoyed executions, no matter what offence the prisoner had been tried for and would be glad when tomorrow was over. A stay of execution would, he hoped, still arrive.

The next day the town was filling up despite the rain. At an early hour that morning, the drop had already been erected upon the platform that forms the roof of the porter's lodge in front of the prison. Around the iron railing surrounding this platform a drapery of black cloth had been fastened. All the entrances of the town were crowded with all types of vehicles conveying the curious to what they evidently considered a show rather than a solemnity. The spectators came from all parts of the county, and there were many from the adjacent counties of Herefordshire, Worcestershire, Warwickshire, and Staffordshire. In fact, an immense concourse of people had assembled to witness the execution. Among the spectators in front of the prison were many respectable and well-dressed inhabitants, but the vast majority were from the agricultural districts. It was said that many farmers had received entreaties from their servants to let them have a holiday on Saturday, to see the hanging at 12 and go to the circus at two.

People had travelled from far and wide to be in Shrewsbury for the execution. The crowds were estimated to be in the thousands, and the inns were already packed. Outside the gaol, the square was full, as people awaited the execution or the arrival of the Red Rover that might bear a letter from the home secretary to grant a dispensation for clemency.

Minutes later, the Red Rover arrived. There was a surge towards the coach, and the constables had to push the crowds back. Mr Peele, the acting under-sheriff, and Mr David Dawson, governor of the gaol, were at the post office before the arrival of the mail, although neither of them anticipated that mercy would be extended to the prisoner. Unfortunately, there was nothing addressed to the governor and there would, alas, be no reprieve for Josiah Mister. With a heavy heart, the governor was forced to give the signal for the execution to go ahead.

Josiah's cell door was opened, and he was joined by two jailers, a priest, the governor, and the man who had visited him the day before, dressed in a smock frock. The bells started to ring, and Josiah was led to the end of the corridor. The door opened once or twice just for a second, and the crowd caught a glimpse of the prisoner. He wore the same attire he had on during the trial. He turned his face to the door each time that it was opened, as if wished to see who or how many persons were outside. Since the trial, Mister's complexion had turned from a clear olive to very sallow. The muscles under his eyes were swollen from weeping and he held a handkerchief in his hand, which he applied to his eyes at intervals. His hair, which wore combed very much to one side, had strayed out of place, and nearly covered his left eye. His countenance had a deeply sad expression and he appeared calm.

In passing from the vestry to the entry of the turnkey's lodge, the wretched man's funeral procession was formed. It was headed by the Reverend Winstone, who was immediately followed by the prisoner. He walked with a firm step and immediately behind him walked the executioner with other gentlemen behind.

When the party reached the porter's lodge, the prisoner paused, looked at the gentlemen who surrounded him fancying he saw the Jury and asked, "Are these the Jury?" Receiving an answer in the negative, he said, in a faint voice, "I freely forgive the Jury."

He was then assisted up the stairs, walking with a firm step, and followed Reverend Winston into a small room, near the head of the staircase. He knelt down and prayed. He remained here a very brief time, took his leave of the chaplain, and then ascended the few remaining steps that led to where the drop had been erected. With his hands tied, the executioner known as 'The Finisher[10]' placed a hood over Mister's head and led him forward to a platform in front of an excited and loud crowd of thousands.

At five minutes to 12, the prison-bell pealed the death-toll. Mister's shirt-collar was turned down, the fatal rope was placed round his neck, and his arms were pinioned. He was in tears but appeared quite conscious of all that he saw and heard. To the earnest demand on the part of the chaplain, whether he believed in the promises of salvation through the blood of our Lord Jesus Christ, he replied, in a low but audible tone "I do."

At three minutes past noon, a momentary silence swept across the throng of onlookers. Without delay, there was a sharp squeal of a hinge, and then a crash as the trapdoor sprung open, and Josiah Mister was launched into eternity.

The rain began to fall heavily, and the jovial crowds gradually dispersed. The atmosphere was far from solemn; in fact, it was the

---

10. The finisher or Jack Ketch was a common nickname for a hangman.

opposite. The public houses were full, and people were enjoying themselves. Drunkenness was the order of the day.

Back at the gaol, Josiah Mister's body was left hanging for more than an hour before being taken down for examination by a surgeon. His body was stripped of its soiled clothes and the garments given to the finisher, a customary practice of the day. The reason? They could be easily cleaned and sold for a handsome profit should he wish to do so. What one might call a perk of the profession.

The surgeon examined Josiah's body by making several incisions and concluded that his neck had not been broken, but he had died instantly from asphyxiation.

Drinking in the town went on well into the night, and the hangman was among the drinkers. He had already been made good offers for items of Josiah Mister's clothing, but he had turned them all down, knowing he could get a lot more elsewhere. The following morning, he left Shrewsbury, passing the prison where the scaffold was being dismantled until the next time it would be required. He was heading to Bridgnorth to conduct some business before heading home to Stourbridge, where he had a business as a cutler.

Two days later, an extraordinary incident was reported in Bridgnorth when a Constable Edwards was called to apprehend a drunk. The crowd surrounding the man were calling "Jack Ketch! Jack Ketch!" The man was then arrested for being drunk and disorderly and taken to the police station to be charged and identified. There was a letter in his possession and 35 shillings he had received for the hanging of Josiah Mister.

The letter was from the governor of Shrewsbury gaol, with these words:

Sir, you had better come over to Shrewsbury immediately, as the planned execution of the condemned prisoner is due to take place this coming Saturday.
Yours faithfully,
Mr David Dawson, Governor, Shrewsbury Gaol.

There was also a bundle of clothes wrapped in a filthy rag, believed to have belonged to Mister.

During his overnight stay in the lockup, several people visited him out of curiosity and offered large sums of money for any portion of the precious wardrobe, but he declined them all.

His identity was confirmed, and the following morning he was brought before the magistrates and fined the sum of 60 pence before being sent back home to Stourbridge. Unfortunately, his ability as a cutler was hampered by drink and work dropped off. He died five years later in Kidderminster.

Before his death, while sitting in his cell, Josiah Mister had written a final letter to his family and his fiancée, continuing to claim his innocence. In the same letter he also complained about his prison diet. The standard for all prisoners was two and one-quarter pounds of best bread, three pints of oatmeal gruel, one pound of boiled potatoes, water, and a pint of ale, to be served three times a day.

After the hanging, Josiah's jailers reported that in his last hours he had engraved on the back of his tin plate with a piece of glass these words,

Charged with an attempted murder and the cutting of Mr Mackreth's throat on Thursday 20th day of August 1840, at the Angel Inn, Ludlow. In my defence which that Almighty and Great God knows that I am innocent and gives me the fortitude to support myself in this time of trouble. I am well aware that he will not let the innocent suffer for the guilty. I trust in my Maker, for He judges the heart, and I am sure that man cannot be greater than God in judgement. False witness may try to find me guilty, but that Just One will make his testimony of no avail. Therefore, reader, trust in God when you are in trouble, and He will ever be your supporter.

Josiah Mister, Birmingham.

The tin plate was later sold for a large profit. The body of Josiah Mister is buried along the north side of St Mary's Church in Shrewsbury, a stone's throw from where he was hanged. Josiah Mister was the last man to hang in England for attempted murder, with the practice later abolished in 1861.

William Miller Mackreth.
(*By permission of Shrewsbury Archives*)

Josiah Mister.

The Angel Inn, Ludlow. (*By permission of Shrewsbury Archives*)

Unicorn Inn, Shrewsbury.

The Angel Inn today.

The window in William's Mackreth's room
at The Angel Inn.

Shrewsbury Jail where Josiah Mister was hanged.

The hanging of Josiah Mister watched by thousands of onlookers.